Acknowledge

I would like to thank my dad, Michael, for encouraging me to write from when I was little, and for giving me some great feedback when he read my first draft. I also want to thank Ms Cashell, my English teacher, who nurtured my love of stories, both reading and writing them. Thank you to everyone who read my first edition - and for pointing out some little glitches! I would especially like to mention Alice, who prompted me to write an extended edition.

Table of Contents – Part One

Into the Mire

Last day of my exams - such a relief! I have been studying insanely for the past year, and when I say insanely, I really do mean INSANELY. I'm pretty certain my hair is going to start falling out now that the stress is relieved, because the tension must have held it on my head while I was tearing it out (or trying). School is not particularly a success story in my case, at least not socially. I am not really the popular type, although I do achieve very good exam results.

I plonk my handbag down on the sofa and quickly start making dinner - being half starved from forgetting my lunch of course. You may be wondering where all my family is - my parents died when I was three months old, but... I just feel like they are still alive. That they had some reason to stay away, almost like they wanted to protect me. I never got an explanation of how they died - I don't think my Aunt Skifa actually knows. My aunty does not have such a great maternal instinct, and certainly doesn't relish the concept of me living anywhere near her. She just helped me find a flat in town near my school at the start of the school year. Oh, and yes, I had to pay for it using the money from my weekend/ summer job and my inheritance - which I just got when I turned eighteen recently.

It's great sometimes - and not so great at other times. For example, it's sometimes lonely. I always felt like my family is out there in the big wide universe, just waiting for me to come home. In fact, to tell the truth, I never felt at home here on earth. I have always been so different to all of my peers. More intelligent, above the average in information retention compared to others my age. Aunt Skifa dismissed my abilities for most of my life, telling me to stop reading encyclopaedias and talking constantly about fanciful inventions.

Suddenly, I snap out of my reverie, remembering that I am completely alone in my apartment. My fight or flight instinct never really became dimmed as with everybody else on this planet. Their nonchalance is insufferable. Sometimes, I get the sense that somebody else is in the apartment, ambushing me...

Like now.

I feel the hairs at the back of my neck rising. An icy chill courses through my central nervous system. There are two of them, certainly. They are whispering almost indecipherably to each other. They have to be on the balcony. This time it's real. It's real, and is certainly unearthly. Almost like they know who I am. Like they can read my mind.

Creeping cautiously towards the sliding patio door, I pause, pressed against the wall. Suddenly, I hear an overpowering voice, commanding:
   "Come to the glass door structure. Do not be afraid. We know you, but you do not know us. If you do not respond, we will enter the interior of the building."
Being at this stage extremely freaked out, I decide to obey. After all, I am taller than most people in this country. I might just be able to scare them off... it usually works with the classroom bullies. It is hilarious to see their faces when I tower over them...

   'We are aware of your stature. Now, um, please come to your glass door.'

Yep, definitely scared now. What even was that? It felt like a thought, but sounded like a voice. I sidle anxiously towards my door with my hands in the air. As the assailants come into view, I almost smash the glass in terror. They are huge, much taller than anybody I have ever seen. Well, that is apart from me. Dressed entirely in black, with only their piercing heterochromia eyes glaring out. 'Calm down now Jasmine, the Mafia isn't coming to get you. Or are they?'

   "Who are you?" I demand.
   "We are the Illumaens."

A sharp sting, then unfeeling darkness.

I awake suddenly with a piercing pain in my right arm. Glancing to determine the cause, I see a very strange device which has some sort of coding on it. Looking around me, I observe that I am sitting in a bizarre room. There are two monstrous Gothic style doors on each side, with cast iron handles. There is a sense of nobility about this place. I kind of recognise it from dreams I used to have when I was little. There was often a man standing at the door, looking at me. It used to really scare me. I appear to be sitting at a highly elongated table, rectangular in geometry, with many chairs on either side. The furniture is so highly polished that I can almost see my reflection in the ebony hued wooden surface. I decide to get up and investigate. Suddenly, a high-pitched beep emanating from the device. Then... nothing.

Again, I revive. Only this time there is rather a stern looking person glaring severely at me. Just - why? I've never had a dream that just re-began with such continuity. Well, I am almost positive that this is indeed a dream. He does not look like the other man in my previous dreams though...

"*Polypterus Senegalis*, greetings," he declares. "Welcome, fellow member of the Society."

"Um, which society are you referring to?"

"Well, of course the Illumaen society."

"I am mildly disoriented - how do I qualify?"

"Firstly, you are an Illumaen. You are part of a race of highly rational and logical beings."

"O... kay?"

"Secondly, while you were asleep our technicians ran diagnostics on your brain, and we concluded that your Intelligence Quotient is high enough for you to become a member of the society."

I consider this blatantly odd proposal set before me. A bunch of telepathic tall people has just kidnapped me, and now allegedly I am in their "Society." This place is so strange and foreign, and yet I feel at home… I definitely must have tripped a switch trying to remember the musical features of *Bohemian Rhapsody*. Let's test the extent of my insane vision.

"I am not on the third planet in the solar system, correct?"

"Certainly not. You are on Illuma, of the Rigel system."

"The system on Orion's belt?"

"Indeed."

"Thank you for informing me of this situation."

The person walks up to me and removes the device. He then indicates towards a throne-like chair on a platform beside the table. I follow him up four steps, before progressing around the semi-circular desk structure to the chair.

"I request that you sit here, present leader of our planet. Your intelligence has earned you your station."

He takes out a flute-like instrument and plays a pentatonic scale, modal in tonality.

Suddenly, about forty other Illumaens file in, each expressing a very controlled, logical acknowledgement. Amazingly, despite having little knowledge of this new culture, my Illumaen instincts seem to activate. One of the hallmarks of a dream, I guess, is knowing exactly what to do in a completely crazy situation.

"You may be seated," I announce, simultaneously sitting on my chair. Everybody sits in perfect unison, and gazes expectantly in silence, awaiting further instruction. But strangely I can hear them whispering to one another, asking questions and wondering which motions will be considered today. Well, I am certainly beginning to believe this incredulous dream, it ought not to be some foolish hoax. It is simply too real. I can hear everything, see everything in such vivid detail. Why, I can even touch the chair, and know it is completely solid. It is also pretty comfortable.

"Which motions require the attention of the society today?"

A young-looking woman rises to speak.

"The offensive from the Scytharians has been contained, and so far, our newly innovated food dispensing organisation is proving effective. There is not much else to explain."

"A brilliant status report. Gratitude conveyed." This is my kind of society, so formal and orderly... Even though I have no idea who these "Scytharians" are.

Spontaneously, the edge of the table and the semi-circular desk glows red, and what seems like harp music plays a continuously rising arpeggio.

"Security breach," the stern person who woke me states matter-of-factly. Instantaneously, a very determined looking woman marches in.

"I am Nada of Serpentin. I request a voice in the council."

I look her up and down seriously, examining the validity of her claim. Her body language suggests both that she is from another planet or city, and she seems quite sure of herself. She is dressed almost entirely in black, with the exception of her olive-green crop top. The fact that she has black leather on her person, including her biker style jacket, suggests that she wants to project an independent image. Her confidence in her appearance is remarkable, judging from her black leather skinny leg trousers. She must be in authority, or a rebel, I am not sure which... I suppose that I should give her a chance to explain herself.

"Speak what you must say..."

"I request a brief meeting with Jade Firedancer, the half Illumaen."

"I am unaware as to who this Illumaen is, or of their location."

Presently, one of the society members interrupts my train of thought:

'You are Jade Firedancer.'

Wait, what just happened there? Did someone just communicate with me... without opening their mouth?? Nevertheless, I have no time to ponder over that presently - I must deal with this "Nada," whoever she is.

"Will you please let the society discuss this proposal, Nada?"

"Yes, but you cannot fool a Serpentin."

"Point acknowledged."

At this stage, I am immensely confused. Not that I am not already baffled by all these introductions to interstellar affairs I had no idea existed previously. Nada is escorted outside by a security guard, and the society is once again seated. An older man stands, waiting for permission to explain this strange intrusion. That is him. The man I always used to see staring at me from across the room. I nod in acknowledgement, and he commences his exposition.

"You are Jade Firedancer. Half Illumaen, half Serpentin. I am your father, who named you Jade."

"And what is your name, Father?" That kind of explains why I saw him when I was small. I must have had a vague recollection of his appearance, somehow. My infantile brain just interpreted him as scary for some reason.

"My name is irrelevant. Nevertheless, when you were born, the Serpentins and the Illumaens were at war, so the then leader of Illuma sent you to earth to be adopted until such a time as you could understand who you really are. That time is now."

I pause briefly, computing this cascade of information. I thought up until now that Illumaens were peaceful.

"I thought that Illumaens were a peaceful nation," I continue.

"Correct, we are peaceful. However, the objective of the Serpentins is to conquer all nations that they possibly can. When they launched an offensive, we acted to defend ourselves, as Illuma is a haven for refugee nations. That was the cause of the war."

"Information comprehended. I will now meet with Nada. Society convention adjourned."

Through the door to the left-hand side of me, there is a small chamber, windowless, with silver grey walls, polished black floor, and brilliant white ceiling. I indicate that Nada be brought into this conference room.

"Greetings," I acknowledge as she struts in, her heeled boots clacking on the floor and her straight, shoulder length black hair swaying slightly. Shutting the door, I turn to discover that she has already seated herself strategically with her back to me. I walk around to where I can face her, trying not to be intimidated by her preying stare and very straight cut fringe lying just on her eyebrows.

"Oh, it's you..." she looks semi-disgustedly at me, as if I am simply not good enough to possibly be this "Jade Firedancer."

"It is I."

"So," she commences. "You must understand the predicament we find ourselves in."

"I am simply half Illumaen, half Serpentin. On earth it is not an issue if somebody is half of two races."

"You do not understand." She sounds frustrated now. "Your mother was the Queen of Serpentin, which means..."

"Which means that I inherit her kingdom?"

"Yes, you finally get it," she sighs melodramatically.

"I see. This matter seems more complex than I first considered. I am the leader of two worlds."

"A planet and an empire," Nada interjects.

"Affirmative. In this predicament it would seem logical to relinquish authority in one instance."

"But you are the only heiress to the throne. If you were to interrupt the monarchy, the empire would descend into anarchy."

"Then I must consider my only other option - please wait here momentarily."

I come out of the conference room to find my father waiting for me.

"She asked you to leave the council?"

"No, but I have little choice. Who will assume authority?"

"I will, as the next most intelligent Illumaen. Thank you."

"I congratulate you on your receiving this position."

"In return, I would like you to accept the role as Chief Peace Agent and Ambassador for Illuma. This role carries a lot of weight and responsibility, as you will negotiate with various nations to ensure that the universal constitution is not violated. I trust that you are good with languages?"

"I can learn quickly. It would be an honour to accept this position, but I have to be able to operate remotely, from Serpentin."

"That can be arranged. So this matter is settled, excellent."

"Don't you have to discuss this with the council?"

"No, it is a simple role reversal, and should not cause a huge amount of disruption."

Thereafter, I engage in an intense training program in order to prepare me for my new role as Chief Peace Agent and Ambassador. One week of training on Illuma incorporates equivalent information to a year on earth for me, though this is of course adjusted to accommodate for variations in processing speed. I am bombarded with languages, laws and scientific principles governing Illuma and the surrounding planets. One of the most interesting was a study of the Illumaen Union, an organisation which binds an entire sector of the Galaxy to Illuma. As the Serpentins also feed me information, I am beginning to see just how polar the two cultures are. The Illumaens are rational, the Serpentins more driven by emotions. Illumaens promote peace, Serpentins live off conflict. The task I am faced with is gargantuan, but I hope that I can juggle both roles effectively. I have always been told that I can adapt to my circumstances. I even do this with people, calculating what is acceptable based on a person's background and behavioural patterns.

Two weeks and a day later, my training is complete, and I must go to Serpentin to assume my role as the monarch. On earth we would call this attitude "green," fresh and bursting with new information.

"I must go now. Nada wants me to go to Serpentin to assume the throne. Farewell, Father."

We briefly shake hands before parting ways. It seems that on Illuma the citizens, at least those in authority, do not openly display affection.

Serpentin

Nada and I take an "Automated Spherical Galactic Transporter" to Serpentin, which is in the Alphard system, Hydra constellation. I would prefer to call our transport "The Jet Bubble." But that is only my personal opinion. On the way to Serpentin (travelling at several times the speed of light), Nada explains that my Serpentin name is Hydra, after my mother, and my mother's mother, and... well this is a long-standing tradition in the Serpentin Empire. She explains that only the women rule, and if a son is born, he is drafted into the army at the age of eighteen. This would be the equivalent of thirty-six on earth, but the Serpentins do not age as fast as people on earth, and the planet takes twice as long to orbit Alphard. This is a military planet, quite different to the civilisation on Illuma. Well, if I have any power whatsoever, I should most certainly end the conscription requirement. That is, if the dream doesn't end. I must consider the possibility that I have indeed been kidnapped by aliens, and that I am in fact en route to the planet I am meant to rule.

Getting to Serpentin certainly reaffirms that I am the Empress to be. I have never seen so many hominoids gathered in one place! Nada and possibly fifty thousand Serpentins escort me to the imperial buildings, rather magnificent structures with black and green jewels studded around the circumference of three striking cream coloured domes, with a silver solar powering unit making a neat circle on the top of each dome. Nada and I are received by a rather stately looking Admiral, dressed from head to toe in slate grey, aside from his military decorations, which adorn his waist in varying hues of blue, green and red. He helpfully shows me to my lodgings, which are located in the foremost dome, with a splendid view over the "Platz," the city square.

"You will be attended to for your dress shortly. We shall waste no time in installing you as Hydra."

"Thank you. I am ready when all is organised."

After about three minutes, a servant comes rushing up with several yards of a light material, rich forest green, and a box containing various ribbons and beads.

"I will make you a dress to fit exactly," she promises.

"You must be a remarkable seamstress. I admire your skill."

"Thank you. There is not much appreciation on this planet."

Deftly, carefully, the gentle woman fashions me a stunning floor length gown, with a bottle green satin bodice, and a skirt of the light material. The dress has a sweetheart neck, not the most flattering for my non-existent bust, but I think it suits the silhouette of the waist-accentuating bodice. It is embroidered in silver with a representation of the Hydra constellation. A bit tight, but I suppose that I can breathe a little. The bodice is laced up at the back with a thin silver ribbon, and I am given silver satin heels to match. The different shades of green highlight my Jade green eyes, which change hue with light and mood. Having been catapulted back eight hours on my journey to Illuma, and a further hour getting to Serpentin, I am utterly shattered. But after my dress has been made (which took four hours), it is only five thirty. My "*Installation*," as they call it, is due to take place at seven pm. I thought I might get some rest before such a momentous event.

However, it turns out that I have to get my hair styled and makeup applied. Eventually, after an hour of having my long, wavy, chestnut coloured hair contorted into an intricate five-strand crown braid and the makeup artist applying silver eyeshadow and striking dark red lipstick, along with copious amounts of concealer, I am almost ready. I put a silver necklace with an elegant oval pendant depicting a silver snake with a dark green background on, and another assistant puts a silver snake shaped earring which climbs my earlobe so that the head hangs just on the top of my ear in my left ear. Nada comes up to inspect me before I go out to face the crowds, handing me a tiny microphone-like transmitter and fiddling with my earring. It crackles before she speaks into a twin microphone. Her voice rasps against my eardrum. I reply into my microphone, and she nods, tapping a much more discreet earpiece concealed by her stark black hair, which is draped over her ears in a long bob style.

Now I must walk. The ceremony will be held in the centre of the Platz, which I must reach by walking through the crowds gathered around it. There is a silver carpet, laid out carefully by yet more servants, conveniently leading the way to a large circular platform. Silence descends upon the hoards as I appear at the off-white, highly ornate archway of the building. I can hear the soft tapping of my shoes on the carpet as I walk to the platform. Reaching the platform, my heels clack up three steps to the main stage.

There is a serious looking man, with a tall muscular build, waiting for me. He is holding a silver cushion with green stitching detail, with an elegant silver tiara on it. I stand erectly in the spot I am told I must remain in as he approaches. Lifting the tiara reverently off the cushion, he hands the cushion to a servant. The tiara is exquisite, adorned painstakingly with diamonds, with one green gemstone on the highest point. It glitters and sparkles in the fading light and the lighting on the buildings surrounding us. I can almost feel my eyes widening with the stunning aesthetic of it. The man then commences a speech:

"We are here gathered at the Platz in order to celebrate another generation of our marvellous monarchy. When this sacred tiara is placed upon the head of this proud Serpentin," he gestures towards me, "We will be led into a new era of imperial grandeur. This green jewel, which adorns her neck and this tiara, which we know as jade, represents her power and wisdom in leading our people into new frontiers and conquering further into the galaxy. This leader will now be given a new name, to celebrate the dynasty from which she stems, and will continue to reside in the place of her mother. I announce," he declares as he places the tiara on my head, "That this woman, a Serpentin, will assume the throne of the Hydra dynasty, thus assuming the title of Hydra and Empress. Please display your support for our new monarch."

The Platz erupts into thunderous applause as a single horn plays a stately march to demonstrate unanimous support for me. A servant comes and informs me that now I must say a few words. Still delighted with my tiara, but astounded at my consent to rule a race I know next to nothing about,

I confidently stand up on a further raised platform, and the crowd falls silent in expectation.

"I am most honoured to become your new Empress, citizens of Serpentin. I yet have much to learn concerning your culture and traditions, but I trust that you will pardon my inexperience and help me to lead Serpentin into a grand and bright future. Let us first praise those who first founded Serpentin and created an organised civilisation, who toiled to help the Serpentins of the future." The planet seems to like my impromptu speech so far, as the inhabitants are applauding most enthusiastically. "But now, dawns a new era, and I require everybody's utmost support. Good Night to all."

Following my concise conclusion, I walk back into my lodgings to the tune of monumental applause.

Kasia

Having changed into the elegant silk pyjamas provided for me, a perfect sky blue with striking green foliage motifs, I recline regally on a chaise lounge. A perfect evening for a new Empress. There are various literary texts and books relating to the Serpentin government and the traditions associated with the Empire, as it is termed. Opening one, I begin to read, but am easily distracted due to my recent escapade. My tiara sits on a glass table, between the chaise lounge and a two-seater chair. Exhausted and surprisingly hungry, I rise and wander into the kitchen, hoping to find some form of food. Upon arrival, I am confronted with a small figure, very slight, who appears to be shaking. It is a hominoid girl, with gorgeous flowing dark brown hair, tinged with red, reaching to her waist. 'This must be one of the Admiral's daughters,' I think to myself. 'But her body language suggests that she is not proud, like other Serpentins. In addition, she is not dressed as richly as expected.' She is wearing plain white shirt and sky-blue straight leg trousers, reminiscent of the attire of the servants at my *Installation*.

    "Hello, I am Ja - Hydra. What is your name?"

    "M - My name is, um, Kasia."

    "Are you one of the Admiral's daughters?"

    "No, far from it."

She turns to face me, and stares up at me with tearful grey-blue eyes.

    "Then... who are you?"

    "I am your servant - a prisoner of war. I am Allaaraen. I am here to serve you. What do you want?"

    "Never mind. Kasia, would you like to come and talk to me?"

    "Yes, if that is what you wish." There is a melancholy tinge to her voice.

I lead the way, and Kasia follows timidly behind. She seems so afraid, and I intend to find out why. Maybe it will provide me with some insight into Serpentin culture. I sit on a chair to the left of my chaise lounge, and indicate that Kasia should sit opposite me, in a chair on the other side of the oval glass table standing on a support of silver. The furniture's upholstery is gold, with silver leaf motifs, not unlike those on my pyjamas. Kasia is barely perched on the chair, tense and nervous.

"Kasia, I am wondering why you are so tense? Are you afraid of me?"

"Yes, very much." I can see that, as she is clinging to the chair for dear life.

"Why? Is it because of what you have been told about me?"

"Not about you specifically. I was taken from my home world, Allaara, while I was in the meadow near the palaces. I am the princess of Allaara, and my older sister is the heiress to the throne. I was brought here, and trained to fear my master or mistress, on threat of death."

"I cannot understand this. I am still unfamiliar with the customs on Serpentin."

"If a servant proves dissatisfactory, then their master has the right to kill them, or should I say, eat them."

"What?! You mean to say that Serpentins eat those who displease them?"

"Well, why do you think Serpentins are the most feared nation in the galaxy?"

I pause briefly. No wonder this child is so petrified! She has been told that I am going to eat her... Even more impressive is her rhetorical question with a sarcastically laced tone. My Illumaen tendency for empathy pushes me to search for a way to take her back to her family.

"Tell me a little more about Allaara. What are your people like?"

"We are a peaceful nation, neutral in conflicts and non-aggressive. In fact, we have basically no army, by choice."

"How fascinating. Tell me more."

"We are greatly oppressed by every ruling power in the sector. Currently, the Serpentins and Scytharians are trying to gain control of our natural resources and us. They are continually making threats against us, to kill us, or put us in forced labour camps. The Serpentins have already kidnapped some others and me. Their plan is to break my parents' courage."

"Why?"

"Allaara and its moon Palladium have much to offer in the way of natural resources, which we only exploit to a minimal degree. Our belief system dictates that we must respect our planet as if it were given as a trust to us by the Gods. Serpentins and Scytharians have no such respect."

"This is terrible: you must be so scared."

"Yes. I have heard of invasions like this, for example with Oplexus. That place was taken without the Oplexus people even having a chance to fight back."

I will selectively ignore that, as I do not know what or where Oplexus is yet. Nada failed to mention this planet during my rapid crash course in the Serpentin Empire. It must not be overly important to my rule yet.

"If I were to attempt to take you back to your home and family, how would I go about getting you off the planet? Could I simply say that I would like to tour the Serpentin Empire, and that I will take my servant with me?"

"I don't think that will work. They will likely tell you to leave me behind or to eat me first."

"Wait, what did you say they'd ask?"

"That you leave me behind, or eat me first. Serpentins swallow their prey whole, and alive usually."

"Well... is it worth trying the tactic that I wish to prolong your anxiety by taking you off planet before consuming you?"

"I guess it's worth a shot."

"By the way, you should know that I am not leaving the planet without you, and that the guards may ask what you propose they will ask."

Kasia contemplates this insinuation I have proposed. After a moment of pensive silence, she looks in my face, conveying an emotion of trust and gratitude.

"Ok. That is a good plan, Hydra."

"Please call me by my Illumaen name, Jade."

"Right. Let's do this Jade."

I work rapidly, calling for a *Jet Bubble*, and changing into the all grey flying gear Kasia finds for me. Kasia ties her hair back into a tight bun, and slips on some black pumps, like the ones I was given with the flying suit. Adhering to Serpentin custom, I handcuff Kasia's right hand to my left, indicating disfavour, and provide the guards with the explanation I discussed earlier. Soon Kasia and I are exiting the planet's atmosphere, and are on a course for Allaara. It will be four hours before we reach the system Allaara exists in, and so I take the opportunity to rest and also find out about Allaara. I carefully remove the handcuff from Kasia as soon as we are at a steady velocity.

"I'm sorry about the handcuff. Is your wrist sore?"

"No, it's fine!" she laughs. "You are so much more Illumaen than Serpentin. You certainly have the moral inclinations of an Illumaen."

"You do not know how glad I am to hear that, Kasia. So, what's Allaara like?"

"I guess it is a lot like earth, but the atmosphere has twenty-six percent oxygen and seventy-two percent nitrogen, unlike the ratio of twenty-one to seventy-eight. It is covered in meadows, but because of the star we are orbiting, the foliage is blue instead of green. There are many beautiful flowers found nowhere else in the galaxy, and much of these plants are used for nutritional and medicinal purposes. I particularly like the *Zachwyt Kviat,* whose scent brings a feeling of calm and contentment."

"It sounds marvellously beautiful; are there any animals I should know about?"

"There are no predators on Allaara, the Allaaraens included, as we are what earthlings call *Vegan*. However, there are many intricately patterned insects, most with colourful wings or shells, and another animal which you must see before I reveal its name..."

"Look, we are approaching the star system. I think we should slow down a little so I can navigate. So, how old are you, Kasia?"

"On earth I would be ten years old, but on Allaara I am 1.5 years old for every earth year, so I am currently about fifteen years old. I have an older sister who is eighteen Allaaraen years old. She is termed "The Gold Princess," as she is the heiress, and I am "The Silver Princess.""

"How fascinating and highly organised. Is it ok to land in this meadow, close to the city there?"

"Yes, just don't run over the unicorns."

"The what?!" I almost crash land at this revelation. "Unicorns?"

"You heard me correctly Jade. These are the *Unicorns*, which look like the earth Arabian horse, but have a single spiralling horn."
So, Unicorns are not mythical after all, simply alien. I mean, we have Narwhals on Earth, so why not Unicorns here?

We climb out of the *Jet Bubble,* and stand briefly, observing the scene around us. There are several unicorns, all grazing contentedly on the lush blue grass growing copiously in the meadow. Suddenly, a big charcoal grey unicorn, about fifteen hands high, canters to where we are standing. His horn shimmers an intensely metallic silver, with only a single gold thread of colour progressing around the spiral. His mane and tail are a striking matte silver, a shade darker than his horn, with single silver hairs interspersed throughout his mane and tail, resulting in a gentle sheen. As he stands still, his hooves, the same hue as his horn, gleam in the new morning light. (The Allaaraens are about eight hours ahead of Serpentin.) The graceful creature stretches out his grey muzzle, nudging Kasia tenderly, as if greeting a long-lost friend.

"I haven't seen you in two months," he says, startling me considerably.
"How did you escape from Serpentin? Nobody escapes from Serpentin alive," he inquires.
Kasia replies softly: "This young woman, half-Illumaen and half-Serpentin, managed to smuggle me off the planet. I am eternally indebted to her."

"Hello, my name is Jade, but I am the Serpentin monarch, and am also known as Hydra. What is your name?" Apparently, I just have to talk normally to unicorns, and they reply.

"I am Proximus Centauri, the silver unicorn. That is, Kasia and I chose each other as companions, and thus I obtained this rank. I am second to the gold unicorn, Dach, who is the companion of Alina, the gold princess. Our hierarchy is quite complicated, but to render it simply, we occupy the same rank in Unicorn society as our companions in Allaaraen society."

"I am honoured to meet you Proximus."

"Let us go at once to my parents, I must inform them of my return."

Gone is the timid, nervous Kasia I have thus far known, replaced rather spectacularly by a strong, authoritative young woman. She leaps on Proximus' back and beckons me to join her. Soon we are racing, much faster than any ordinary horse, towards the white watchtowers coming into view.

Allaara

We slow to a walk as Proximus' hooves clack confidently on the beautiful beige, red and brown cobblestones of the main city. Knee high water fountains catch the sunlight and glow a gentle, pure pink along the pathways. Cheerful children stroll past leading what appear to be Shetland ponies, but who have silver and gold in their hair and a silver or gold pattern on their hind quarters, depicting leaves, flowers or other decorative motifs. Kasia and I dismount and Proximus leads the way to the main residence. It is a geometrically precise building, with one large central cube and three smaller cubes on three of its sides, excluding the side the door is situated upon. On the top of the central cube is an elliptical room, its sides a gleaming metallic blue in contrast with the white of the rest of the building. "This is the Palace, my home." Kasia smiles.

As we walk through the tall, metallic gold coloured doors, Proximus wheels around and says: "I cannot come in. However, I will inform Dach of your presence." The main hall is stunning, with marble pillars of an ivory hue, having a rich green plant similar to Ivy climbing them to the ceiling. The floor is a striking red marble, which I am informed is found on Allaara's moon, Palladium, and the walls are painted a warm French grey. The two smaller cubes, of equal size, on either side of us, are the sisters' rooms. "Mine is on the left," explains Kasia. "You can tell because it was built more recently than Alina's. Allaaraen law states that rooms must be built as necessary, according to the size of the family. All residences begin as having one bedroom."
At the farthest side of the building, facing us, is the door to the King and Queens' room. This room is slightly bigger than the princesses' rooms, as it was built first.

Suddenly, a woman wearing a rosy pink, flowing floor length gown runs to greet us. She is in her early thirties, and then proceeds to greet Kasia in a way which denotes a mother-child relationship.

"My dearest Kasia, you have returned! I have missed you sorely, and worried incessantly for your welfare in that awful place Serpentin. How did you escape?"

"May I first introduce my recently acquainted friend, Jade. Mother, she managed to smuggle me off planet, and I am eternally indebted to her."

"Why, hello Jade. My name is Sara. Jade is not a typical Serpentin name, how did this anomaly occur?" she beams in greeting, her shoulder length brown hair moving with her enthused head movements.

"Hello, um, Queen Sara. I am pleased to meet you. I am half Illumaen, but I have been appointed to rule Serpentin, so I was on the planet when I met Kasia. I used my high authority to persuade the trust of the guards, so I could take Kasia off the planet as my 'servant.' My Serpentin name is Hydra, but I much prefer to be called by my Illumaen name."

"You can just call me Sara. Now, usually if a Serpentin Empress turns up on our planet, it is time to start panicking because the army is close behind. But you actually rescued my daughter! Serpentins would ordinarily hold her for ransom, but you brought her back. This is an occasion to celebrate."

Beckoning one of the palace servants, Sara announces: "We will hold a special lunch in honour of Kasia and the one who brought her back to us." After an eruption of applause, the servants scurry to prepare for the celebrations. Kasia promptly goes and changes out of her servant's attire, and returns wearing a rich pink dress whose light material reaches to her ankles. The dress has a high round neck adorned with colourless crystals, and is sleeveless. A style which befits both her rank and the planet she lives on. A servant then hands me a soft French grey dress, with a similar neckline ornamented with crystals. Having put it on, it is knee length and of the same material as the others' dresses. I sweep my hair into a neat ballerina bun, and Kasia lends me some silver flower hair decorations with which to add a little sparkle. "My sister has some silver shoes with a jade stone ornamenting them. They should fit you, and will complement the colour of your eyes." As it happens, they do fit, and then, as we are completely decked out for this occasion, we decide to go and find Alina.

Using a blanket so we do not ruin our dresses with unicorn hair, Kasia mounts Proximus and I mount a sweet white unicorn mare named, in rather an earthly fashion, Daisy. There aren't even any daisies on Allaara!

"We will probably find Alina in the west meadow. She was beside the Sapphire Stream last time I saw her, with Dach," surmises Proximus. We decide to take a leisurely trot out to the west meadow, where the mid-morning drizzle is dusting the landscape. The west meadow is substantially more diverse than the north meadow (the directions are according to the location of the main city of Allaara), with many hues and shapes of flower scattered across the grass. Soon the deep blue stream comes into view, and a little away, across the stream, is a magnificent golden coloured Unicorn, with a thread of red running through his metallic gold horn and red hairs interspersed throughout his mane and tail, like the silver in Proximus' mane and tail.

"Alina!" Kasia calls out. "I have returned finally. I have with me Jade, the Illumaen Proximus told you about."
Soon a slim girl, a little taller than Kasia, emerges from behind the lone, spread-eagled tree visible beside the stream. As we cross the stream to meet her, her striking platinum blond hair gleams in a manner which catches the sunlight. She has the same expressive, intense eyes as her sister, only hers are a dazzling electric blue. She carries herself nobly, as a princess would, though not snobbishly.

"Sister! I am elated to see you once more," she exclaims, running over and hugging Kasia. "I picked some *Zachwyt Kviat* for you."

"Thank you!" Kasia enthuses, inhaling the heavenly scent of the delicate white flower, almost transparent with pure beauty.

"I will be ready soon," Alina remarks as she mounts Dach, quickly thundering into the distance towards the city. (Kasia kindly translated from Allaaraen Szaen, a language not dissimilar to the earth language of Polish.)

Soon the royal family, two young generals and I are seated in the rather grand upper room, the roof being entirely constructed from metallic blue glass (I am told it is more energy efficient), and the floor being white marble. At this point I have not eaten in twenty-four hours, and am endlessly grateful when the food comes. I am just admiring the gorgeous presentation and the luscious scents when my earring projects a voice from Illuma:

"Jade Firedancer, we require that you peregrinate to earth in order to negotiate a peace treaty with the Scytharians. They refuse to meet elsewhere. This order takes effect immediately."

"Understood. I will make arrangements at once," I fumble for the microphone before replying as calmly as possible.
How did the Illumaens gain access to my earring? It must have been a condition of them allowing me to go to Serpentin. Well, at least Illumaens are less irritating than the voice of Nada hissing at me.

"I regret to inform you that I have urgent matters to attend to. Please convey my compliments to your remarkable chef, and I thank you for your hospitality. I must warn you, that in the little time I had to gather military information from Serpentin, I discovered that they will soon begin raiding in order to capture Alina. Send her somewhere safe, or I will be forced to torture and execute her. I will not be able to communicate in the meantime. I only hope that your peaceful society will continue to thrive."

"Thank you for your timely warning Jade. It will always be a pleasure to welcome you to our city. Farewell."

With that I ride Daisy to the *Jet Bubble*, and set a direct course for earth. She nickers softly at me as I climb into the *Jet Bubble*;

"Farewell Jade. I hope that I may see you again at some point."

"I hope so too."
Strange how you are invariably sent back to where you came from.

Earth and Its Assorted Sub-Sectors

I reach Earth in the evening, just after sunset. Landing carefully at the edge of the Empty Quarter of Saudi Arabia, I step out once more onto the planet of my youth. Setting the *Jet Bubble* on Autopilot to return to Serpentin, I take a veritable leap of faith. I have no transport, and I am surrounded by almost featureless desert. I must reach Dubai to discuss the treaty with the Scytharians by the next morning.

Earth is a planet divided amongst itself, possibly the most divided of all the planets in the Galaxy. The earthlings divided it first into six "continents," large landmasses or areas of territory. I am in the "Asia" continent presently. Then, the continents are sub-divided into "countries," parcels of land which are constantly at war with each other, often due to resources or a territorial notion of "borders." This conflict is particularly prevalent in this sector, with a number of countries within the Asia continent dubbed "The Middle East." Perhaps this is why the Scytharians chose to meet here: the citizens of Dubai are too busy worrying about other matters to be concerned with the concept of extra-terrestrials.

Wading a few kilometres through the searing sand, I arrive at the nearest settlement, grateful for my top-quality Illumaen GPS (Galactic Positioning System). Purchasing a four-wheel drive truck designed for off-roading, I power over the sand dunes until I locate a road. I drive incessantly through the night. Unfortunately, humans have not yet developed overly efficient engines, and so I am forced to travel at a mere earth eighty kilometres an hour. (This measurement is equivalent to a miniscule fraction of the *Jet Bubble's* speed, to the approximate order of 7×10^{-8} galactic light jumps per second. An Automated Spherical Galactic Transporter travels at two galactic light jumps per second.) I reach Dubai by sunrise, successfully disposing of my transport in order to pay for lodgings in one of the city's numerous gleaming skyscraper hotels. The metal and glass make this city even hotter than the desert outside, although the shadows of the skyscrapers provide a little respite. It does not help that Saudi women must wear a Hijab and Abaya, a garment which covers her down to her ankles - excellent protection from the sun, but quite warm in some cases.

I am to meet with the Scytharian ambassador at ten a.m. earth time. Having not eaten in three days, I go to find some kind of breakfast. Despite looking through a dictionary and phrase book on the way to earth, my Arabic is not the most monumentally astounding. Besides, I have to communicate with the Scytharians in Scythaon, their empirical language, and must get into the correct mind set. I pick up a pomegranate and some dates on the way to early check in at the hotel that I am to meet the ambassador at. I have no idea what to expect...

At precisely ten a.m., the ambassador arrives in a rather stately fashion, along with two aides who quite blatantly carry concealed weapons - you can tell from their guilty looks. I glance up from my book concerning Serpentin custom to inspect them. They are perhaps only about five foot two, with the ambassador only slightly taller at five foot four. I was told to predict this stature, as it is a part of their genetic composition. He is wearing what appears to be an attempt at a suit, which truly does not complement the heavy awards he displays around his neck. "Greetings from the Scytharian Empire," he announces pompously in Scythaon.

"Greetings from Illuma, and the Illumaen Union. I am Jade, Ambassador for peace."

"You may refer to me as Trajod, Ambassador and Personal Adviser to the Emperor."

"Accepted Trajod."

"Now, for business. Why have you requested this ultimately pointless meeting?"

"I wish to advise the Emperor not to declare war on Illuma. It is unwise to deliberately interfere with our trade and airspace."

"Your advice means nothing to us. We are an entirely independent empire, and will not hesitate to conquer strategic planets to expand our influence."

"I must warn you, that planets which rely on Illuma will also not falter in their resolution to protect the other members of the Union, which includes Illuma. Your proposed decision is unwise."

"I will not listen to your foolish intuitive ravings. You speak like a true Illumaen - so logical you fail to see the advantages of keeping your mouth shut. We will simply go to the Hydra of Serpentin to propose an entire invasion. Serpentins are so feared the planets will easily cower before us."

"I would not rely solely on the Serpentins. Their new leader is striving for empirical stability, not further conquest."

"How would you know? Your mind-reading does not extend this far."

"Perhaps I know something that you do not, and you certainly would dislike its revelation."

"It that a threat, Jade?" he quips sarcastically.

"No, Trajod. However, I see that this meeting is not progressing in a constructive manner. I warn that diplomacy is far better than combat."

"Let combat occur! I officially declare war on Illuma and the Illumaen Union."

Boy, are these Scytharians easily riled. How can one possibly reason with such a people?

"Please, I ask you to retract your statement..."
"Never! Execute her, slaves!"

With that the two aides reveal their Scytharian bows, equipped with very short but instantly fatal arrows. I have read about them, under the section "deadly weapons" in the Illumaen Diplomatic Handbook. The military undergo intensive training in order to properly utilise these. Fight, flight, or freeze? Flight is the most logical action. I cannot believe the attitude of the people around me... they seem entirely blasé regarding this entire situation. Quickly rising, I head directly for the stairs (having the dining area on the fourth floor now has enormous disadvantages). One of the servants wields a short dagger, stalking me with a movement reminiscent of a fiddler crab of the mangrove forests on earth. The other draws his bow and attempts to take shots at me, which I successfully evade before slamming the door in their faces. I peregrinate rapidly down the eight flights of stairs to reach the ground floor, resisting the urge to kick the door open dramatically. The danger draws closer, like the tension on the bows. The receptionist barely has time to tell me not to hurtle outdoors without my headscarf when the aide with the dagger floors her, threatening to kill her if she does not remain silent. The other, whom I will call Alpha for simplicity, has blocked the door. The arrow is pointed directly at my temple. If he shoots, there will only be a millisecond before consciousness ceases...

Too late. That stupid receptionist screams like a screech owl, before promptly taking an arrow from Alpha. My chance for liberty! Dashing frantically towards the distracted Alpha, I startle him considerably. Abayas have their limitations when one is trying to defeat a Scytharian. Fortunately, his bow has been knocked out of his reach. Picking it up, I rapidly assess it. Being Illumaen results in an incredible mental processing speed and ability to obtain and retain information. Drawing it in the manner that Alpha utilised it, I direct it at his head...

"Please, no!" He screams rather childishly at me.
"Then leave, you and your so called "Ambassador.""
"Yes, yes, absolutely!"
He turns to the Ambassador and Beta. Previous to this, Beta had been approaching supposedly stealthily with his dagger. He stops dead, turns to Trajod, and receives a nod. Then, without a word, they simply leave. Courteously, I beam beatifically while handing the Scytharian Bow back to Alpha.
"Now, leave this planet before the whole of Dubai turns against you."
"Understood."

29

Well, I doubt very much that they will be returning any time soon.

Russia; Continent of Europe/Asia

My flight to Moscow is booked for the following morning. I take the day in Dubai to wander around, observing the people and generally re-adjusting to the gravity of earth. It is rather strange to simply remain in one city, completely independent of transmissions (I cannot send any due to the Scytharians watching the space sector above Dubai). I have not been settled for two earth days now. I had quite forgotten how beautiful a thing stasis is. I decide to learn Russian that evening, having eaten a four-course meal. I find the characters intriguing, but nonetheless comprehensible. Eventually, I fall asleep, utterly exhausted from the past two days. Sleep, I have concluded, is more valuable than Platinum. I still half-expect to wake up in my own bed in the morning, but, of course, that is not so. I am acclimatising to this new reality slowly but surely. I do not mind it so much. Very different, but not unbearable.

At ten fifteen Dubai time, I am on a flight to Moscow. What shall I do when I reach there? I have never been to Moscow before. I have always considered going, to experience the architecture and culture of the city. The first task is of course to inform Illuma and Serpentin that I haven't vanished from the universe into a different dimension (You must believe; it is most feasible). Perhaps a little shopping is in order... after all, I have only my flying outfit and my Abaya. Time for a new look, one perchance a little more like both worlds rather than simply one. For the rest of the flight, the person situated beside me falls asleep, snoring most intolerably while hard rock booms from their headphones. Most unbefitting for an Empress and Ambassador. Especially as this Empress and Ambassador must revise Russian, and continue studying the customs of Serpentin.

Touchdown is at two ten, slightly early. Planes also do not travel very quickly, in comparison to a *Jet Bubble*. I suppose I was accustomed to it for years while living on Earth. Yet, how different two days can make a mode of transport. Walking out of departures, I immediately progress towards my accommodation for the evening, a four-star hotel which appears to be acceptable, based purely on reviews by previous customers. Moscow is strikingly different to Dubai - less glass and skyscrapers, more ornamented buildings and monuments. In addition, it is a welcome relief to see some genuinely green foliage, not irrigated flowers in the midst of the desert. The people are also worlds apart - suited businessmen hurrying past, and a group of young women hanging around wearing shorts, showing off their long slim legs: there is not an Abaya in sight. Except for me. I quickly rectify the situation, changing into the grey flying outfit which to the terrestrial appears to be a form of tracksuit.

Having settled satisfactorily in my hotel room, I make contact with both Illuma and Serpentin. Illuma bears an urgent communication informing me that the war has begun:

"We have informed the rest of the Union, and the situation is in hand."

"Excellent. I am currently in Moscow, sub sector Russia, sector Europe of Earth. Please contact me further if you require me. Thank you."

"Understood. Farewell."

By this time, the Chief Admiral of Serpentin is bellowing down my earpiece, impatient to tell me about the latest military developments:

"Greetings Hydra."

"Greetings Admiral," I speak into my hand-held microphone.

"We have raided Allaara and its moon Palladium, but have failed to capture the Gold Princess. They may seek refuge on earth, we will send agents to eliminate her soon, after they scour the rest of the systems surrounding Allaara."

"Thank you for this information. I can assure you that I will most certainly eliminate that roguish in-subordinating traitor to the empire. Then the King and Queen will be forced to bow under our yoke. Farewell."

A click, and once more I am alone. In glorious silence as I saunter down the stairs to exit the hotel. People passing pleasantly. Asking for directions at the three-person reception, I make my way towards the shopping centres and boutiques of Moscow. Such vast variety and colour even in the shop fronts, a respite from the clinical silver of Dubai's skyscrapers. I weave and meander in and out of shops, examining the wares and attempting to construct a coordinated outfit. If one were to look at a map of Dubai and Moscow side by side, it is clearly evident that Dubai is relatively new and grid-planned, a little like New York. Moscow, however, is older, and is subject to urban sprawl. Endearing in some aspects, older cities carry with them a certain aura of antiquated charm. I only see the famed domes of the Orthodox Church from a distance: Perhaps I will get an opportunity to sightsee tomorrow. Colour on the skyline. Sunset descending softly. Beautiful brushstrokes on the palette of the dusk sky.

Chromium: The Theory of the Universe, and other Matters

Finding a convenient bathroom, I change into my successfully purchased outfit: A black leather effect jacket with a gold zip and gold pocket details. My selected top is a black V-neck t-shirt with a glittering motif of repeating diagonal waves. Each point of colour alternates between gold and silver. To complete the look, I matched some leather effect slim leg trousers with gold zips on the pockets and some black shoes with a small heel. Surprisingly comfortable. Exiting with my flying suit stashed in my shopping bags, I head back in the direction of the hotel, a fifteen-minute walk. After five minutes I adjust to people turning their heads as I continue with purpose down the street. But nothing prepared me for what happened next...

There are what I can only describe as a gang of five bikers standing by their transports staring at me. Nodding at them regally, I pursue my goal of the hotel. Suddenly, one stands out in front of me.

"Hey babe," he drawls annoyingly in Russian.

"Hello. Get out of my way please."

"Nah. Come take a ride with us. (He gestures towards his Harley and the other bikers) Where do you want to go?"

"Nowhere with you lot. Goodbye."

He grabs my arm and pulls me uncomfortably close.

"You don't get away with looking that good in my city. Not when you are single too."

"She's taken, let her go losers," a voice behind me demands. Turning my head cautiously, I see the trademark heterochromia of an Illumaen.

"I'd let go if I were you. He is better trained in martial arts than the CIA and KGB combined." I finish off my statement with a mischievous smile. The bikers seem suitably taken aback by this.

"Sure man. Sorry 'bout your girlfriend. She's just too hot to leave alone. Take her." He shoves me towards the Illumaen, saying; "Let's go boys, we don't want any trouble."

With that, all five of them leave quickly, revving their engines and disappearing in a cloud of smoke. I turn to the Illumaen:

"How did you know I was Illumaen?"

"I saw you from far away, and glimpsed your intelligence. You must be close to the top of Illumaen society."

"I am the chief agent for peace and Ambassador."

"Oh, you're *that* Illumaen. Agent 625. 5 to the power of four."

"I was not aware that I had a number."

"All of the agents have a number. You have a perfect quartic number, indicating intelligence which is higher than your station," he looks intently at me, with his perceptive, gentle eyes, one dark brown, and one hazel.

"Thank you. What is your name, and what rank do you occupy?"

"I am Chromium. I am a researcher of quantum science and chief professor of scientific research on Illuma. My aptitude for physics and science is the highest on Illuma, with you second, only ten points behind. I have great respect for your intelligence."

"Quite impressive credentials. I hope that I was not lying when I mentioned your combat training."

"No, that was my personal project a couple of years ago when I first became chief scientist at the age of eighteen. All Illumaens are assigned a post based on their aptitudes when they reach the age of eighteen."

So that's why I was only kidnapped when I had been eighteen for a while... I was trying to figure that out.

"Fascinating. Are you aware of my Serpentin blood?"

"Yes. A formidable combination in an Ambassador. The Serpentin instinct for militaristic strategies combined with the logic of an Illumaen is almost undefeatable. Are you trained in martial arts?"

"No, but I participate in contemporary dance combined with strength training, which makes me well able to defend myself."

"A logical conclusion, although you should consider learning a little of the martial arts - they are extremely useful. Should we go and have dinner at our hotel? It is approximately the time when humans eat."

"I was just heading for there when I was intercepted by those thugs." He mentions the name of the hotel, and I discover, surprisingly, that we both selected the same hotel.

"Well, evidently we based our choice on the same demographics," Chromium states matter-of-factly.

"Evidently," I muse as we both recommence our journey back to the hotel. There are thousands of people in this city, and by some cosmic chance the only two Illumaens meet. Perchance those who look for signs will find some meaning in this.

We sit at a table in the corner with a large window gazing out upon the city lights at the restaurant on the second floor. The light from the three chandeliers placed in a linear formation along the length of the ceiling bathes the red and gold themed décor in a soft glow. I feel underdressed for the occasion; Chromium is wearing a black suit with a white shirt and silver tie. At least I can find refuge in the fact that I did not know that this was going to occur. After an attractive waitress with bobbed black hair takes our orders, we have time to study one another. Chromium has an unnaturally straight and defined jawline, and a prominent brow ridge. His eyes are slightly further apart than the scientific "perfection" measurement, but remain in proportion with the rest of his face. They shine as he gazes, a wise, discerning eye contact holding my attention. His nose is slightly larger than would be expected, and his eyebrows are very straight and precise, with a short tail angled down, as if to denote his scientific inclination. I catch him also analysing me, his eyes flitting and tracking as he calculates the shape of my face and the organisation of my features. I can hear his train of thought, running through algorithms to logically process my appearance.

"You were also analysing me, yes?" he comments.

"Yes, your thought runs quickly."

"Your thought is about the same speed. It develops from the Illumaen intelligence."

"Which theories are you currently working on?"

"Wow, that is rather forward of you! At the moment I am pondering over the theory of why superconductors behave in the manner that they do. I seem to have narrowed it down to the quantum level, but am still working on what exactly causes the phenomenon."

"Surely the reason is because the molecules in a superconductor react with the quanta surrounding them, causing them to become ionised and magnetised simultaneously. This results in electrons being able to flow at astounding rates through the superconductor."

"Exactly. This is the most flawless explanation that I have heard for superconductivity since I first selected the concept for study. This theory is revolutionary, with many applications in transport systems between galaxies and star systems. I will be sure to mention your name when I publish the hypothesis."

"Gratitude. I am glad to be of assistance during your quest for scientific discovery."

At that moment the waitress returns with our main course (we mutually decided that starters were a needless waste of time). We spend the rest of our dinner discussing the culture of Illuma and some of the various customs that they have over delicious vegetarian food. Another incredible coincidence; that we are both vegetarians. Then again, many Illumaens are.

"Goodnight. I shall see you tomorrow," I bid farewell to Chromium as we reach the elevator to go up to my room.

"Goodnight... only one small query."

"Yes?"

"Are you willing to enter into camaraderie with me?"

"Of course. You are a rational educated Illumaen whose company I enjoy. Thank you for asking me rather than assuming."

"You are welcome. I wish to express my gratitude for accepting me in friendship. My room is on the third floor, I must go. Farewell my friend."

"Farewell my friend," I repeat as the doors close and the elevator is pulled up to the sixth floor, where my room number is incidentally 625. Another uncanny occurrence of the day.

Once more, it is comforting to lie back on the welcome white sheets of a bed and fall asleep, having had another most fruitful day.

The next morning, I wake approximately five minutes before my alarm, set for 6:30, as is the custom for me. My internal clock is highly adaptable and I have excellent orientation in space and time. Breakfast is from seven to nine here, and I must check out before ten o' clock this morning. Digging around in my shopping bags for something to wear, I lay out my attire on my bed before having a refreshing shower - sometimes one can rate a hotel by its shower, and this shower was quite high in the rankings. Anyway, it is quite unintelligent to talk about a shower constantly. By seven I am drying my hair and pulling on some light blue high-waist jeans. I am sure I can hear some form of kerfuffle outside my door. Probably kids roaming the corridors. Their parents really should supervise them a little more. A whisper of "let me in" is heard, but again, children are strange creatures. They seriously think that I am going to let them in. Besides, I technically shouldn't be able to hear them, due to the music on my phone being turned up to a fairly loud volume. This superhuman hearing is irritating at times.

I pick up a pale green t-shirt with an embroidered heart motif to put on when instantaneously Chromium kicks the door open, ninja style.

"Put your hands u..." he trails off as he sees that I haven't disappeared off the face of the earth.

"Would you mind shutting the door please, I after all am not quite dressed yet."

"Of course," he says, looking me up and down, shutting the door behind him. I swiftly slip the top on while his back is turned.

"Well, that got me ready sooner rather than later," I state dryly.

"I thought that you had been assassinated or something. I was concerned for your wellbeing."

"I appreciate your concern. Nonetheless, you must know that breaking down doors and picking locks is not the way to valiantly protect your newfound comrade. I admire your Illumaen loyalty, although please do not enter my hotel room without my consent again."

"Apologies Jade. I was quite surprised to see you... as you were when I entered. I thought that you would be ready within minutes of waking."

"Perhaps you may be able to pull that feat off, but traditionally a woman needs a little more time to prepare for the day. Just a moment..."

I fasten my black shoes and toss on my jacket. "Now, I *am* ready" I say with a little flair in my tone. Thus, we then go down to breakfast, an acceptably organised buffet style, similar to the concepts utilised in Illumaen accommodation buildings (that is the Illumaen term for a hotel).

Having checked out at precisely five to ten, Chromium and I set off through the streets of Moscow to do a spot of sightseeing, I carrying my luggage over my shoulder in an overnight bag, he pulling a neat grey suitcase behind him. We must look like such tourists. Well, at least we don't look like aliens. Hopefully. As we wander through the streets, I identify a sign advertising a concert regarding the music of Tchaikovsky.

"Do you play an instrument?" Chromium asks.

"I went through my violin grades to diploma level - I completed the last exam the November before this happened."

"I see. I have all the grades required for piano, well at least by earth standards. True virtuoso players are trained intensively for up to twenty years before being labelled competent on Illuma. I also play a variety of other familiar instruments, including the harp, cello, viola, clarinet and saxophone."

"Well… ok. I also sing, and have had a few lessons in classical voice."

"Really? I sing too, I am a tenor."

"I am mezzo soprano or soprano."

"How pleasant."

It seems that Illuma is quite a cut-throat society as far as education is concerned. I feel utterly upstaged by this man, who is only a few months older than me in earth terms. Despite this, it is invigorating to speak on a high level of intelligence, quite changed from the frivolous conversations that were had at school when I was there.

"You aren't by any chance fluent in several languages as well?" I comment with a tinge of sarcasm.

"Actually yes, probably at a similar level to you. I noticed that you adapt your language far quicker than I can. Similar to you, I can read a dictionary and a phrase book in a language and rapidly calculate the grammatical rules, thus enabling me to achieve fluency in a short period of time."

"Much like me reading a Russian dictionary on the plane here and being able to hold a conversation and read signage."

"Exactly."

We come to the landmark which identifies Moscow: the colossal Orthodox Church. The spiralling colours are striking against the blue sky, and the architecture itself is a marvel of art. I never really properly understood why man builds such huge sculpted structures in order to somehow draw closer to a God or powerful entity - who in most cultures condemns greed and vast displays of money as a sin. One of the curiosities of culture, I guess. Having observed that magnificent monument to architecture, I turn back to Chromium, who appears entirely lost in thought.

"What are you pondering over?"

"The very essence of sentience… Apologies, I am in a philosophical mood."

"I was just going to ask if you wish to attend the Tchaikovsky concert."

"Of course. Why, what is there here but music? Only music as the lifeblood of life itself."

"I noted that it is a black-tie event, a terminology on earth referring to the wearing of suits for men and cocktail dresses for women. Do you possess appropriate attire?"

"Certainly."

"I also have acceptable attire, so that appointment is satisfactorily arranged."

"Excellent."

Thus, we arranged to meet outside the concert hall at six o' clock. Chromium turns up wearing a navy suit and a light blue tie. I decide to wear my grey dress, which fitted so well that Sara told me to keep it, accessorized by the silver Allaaraen shoes that Kasia kindly gave me (I wonder if her sister knows). I also wear a silver bracelet I saw yesterday and impulsively bought. I unfortunately have a weakness for shiny objects. I should really wear black and white, due to my magpie-like reputation. Not an overly Illumaen trait. However, I can now put my microphone for communicating with Illuma and Serpentin in my bracelet instead of carried in a small case in my pocket. As we walk in, we are handed an ornate programme, which, is of course, in Russian. "Romeo and Juliet, Fantasy Overture," Chromium and I read simultaneously, startling both each other and those around us. A truly masterful piece of music. My personal favourite of the themes is the strife motif, a kaleidoscope of canons, repeated notes, and an urgent quaver/semiquaver theme at the heart of the motif. I close my eyes and soak in the rich harmonies, melodies and antiphon.

Afterwards, I switch my earpiece on again, and I am greeted by the cacophonous shrieking of Nada. She tells me that Alina (though she did not mention her by name) is on earth. "I'll take care of it, don't concern yourself with this matter," I assure her. I'm going to need all the Illumaen instinct I've got to find Alina and bring her safely to her parents. Peace treaties are so much more practical than empirical warfare. Certainly, Illuma must be the preferred planet for residence.

"What was that?"

"Serpentin. They want me to kill a girl of twelve to achieve the aims of the empire. I am going to propose a rescue mission."

"That is most unfortunate. Did you enjoy the concert?"

"Yes, the strife motif is beautiful, is it not?"

"Yes indeed. I play it on the piano regularly."

"I would love to learn to play the piano. I would be quite sanguine to play the strife motif; it is delightfully dramatic."

"I can teach you if you wish, perhaps when you get back from rescuing the girl."

"That would be wonderful, thank you. The girl's name is Alina, and she is Allaaraen."

"Where are you going to look for her?"

"My instinct tells me that she will seek refuge in Poland, I will go there first."

"May I come with you?"

"If you wish, however Alina may be too nervous to face two people rescuing her."

"Understood." He pauses, as if hesitant to say what is on his mind. I look encouragingly at him, nodding to prompt him. After a moment, he opens his mouth again:

"I can see your propensity for emotion, so a word of warning if I am permitted to give it - be careful Jade, that your emotions do not cloud your judgement."

"I will try to implement this advice. It is much appreciated."

"Farewell for now Jade."

"Farewell Chromium."

With that, I stroll amiably back to the hotel to stay another night, and to book the next flight to Warsaw.

Poland; Continent of Europe

"Witaj!" The woman at the travel desk greets me as I go to find a convenient place to stay. I have only been to Warsaw once before, and it is elating to consider the prospects before me. "Dziękuję," I express my gratitude as I attempt to follow the woman's rapid-fire directions in Polish. Perchance I will learn to understand a little Szaen while here, as my knowledge must be somewhat transferable. Chromium decided to stay in Moscow for a couple more days, so I am once again in solitude. The peace I experience as I walk through the bustling streets is paradoxical, but nonetheless wonderful. Polish people speak extremely quickly, and so I conclude that it may take a little more than reading a dictionary once to recall conversational language. Nevertheless, I read one on the plane, and this time I had quiet to study.

Perhaps you are wondering where I was born. Maybe one day you will find out. However, I shall not divulge that, for that would destroy the utopia of a girl from nowhere. I think that humans place far too much emphasis on race and country of origin; it is a tragic situation.

Checking in at the hotel, I then begin my search. It is paramount that I find Alina before Nada or the military do - especially considering Kasia's revelation concerning executions on Serpentin. Once I have met someone, to a certain extent I can remember their brain patterns. But here, Szaen blends into Polish, because the language patterns are so alike. She will be afraid, unnaturally afraid. Maybe I can work with that. Warsaw is a stunning city, and I particularly like the main square, paved with beige flagstones and surrounded by stone buildings. Reminiscent almost of Allaara, but much more chaotic. The Allaaraens use similar stones to pave their streets. I wander around the immense city for three hours, before finally breaking to eat dinner at 6:30. Perhaps I am wrong - Alina may be looking for me. She is quite intelligent, and knows that I am on this planet. I only hope that she recognises me.

It is dark when I walk back onto the streets of Warsaw. All of the shop fronts are lit with glowing light, inviting the late-night shoppers into their aura of light. Silhouettes in the darkness. Iridescent street lamps, beaming halos of sodium electrons. A place where you know everybody and nobody. Everybody and nobody knows you. A strange and familiar place.

In a moment of epiphany, I see a more than familiar silhouette in the darkness. The small frame, the long hair, the great fear - could it be her? Treading carefully, as if upon eggshells, I approach. She could disappear in an instant: apparitions often do. But is she an apparition? A mere product of my wild imagination? There is only one way to discover the shadow's identity. I think about calling her name - but Alina is a name which is fairly common in these parts. Directly behind her now. Heart pounding in expectation. The ghost turns, and makes eye contact. Will she now dissipate, a projection in my mind?

"Hello?" a small voice whispers softly in my native tongue.

"Hello. I am Jade. Are you lost?" Ok, I hope that did not sound creepy.

"I am Alina. I come from a place a long way from here."

"Do you speak Szaen?"

"Yes, yes I do!" she enthuses in Szaen. "I thought that I recognised you. You are Jade Firedancer, a face I have seen once before. How wonderful it is to see you!"

"Listen, Alina, you have to get off this planet before the Serpentin military get here. Do you need help?"

"Yes. I have no transport."

"Ok, there is a Serpentin coming to accompany me to "search" for you. You must stay close to me, because if Nada finds you before I can take you off-planet... let's not explore that outcome."

"Right, absolutely. How are you going to fool the Serpentin who is coming?"

"Good question... we'll cross that bridge when we come to it."

I had booked a twin room in the accommodation, in case an event like this occurred. My instincts it seems are rather accurate. Alina is cold and exhausted, abandoned in a panic by two Allaaraen diplomats. I tell her that she is free to settle in, before switching my earpiece back on. Nada is on the other end... again. She informs me that the intelligence agent is waiting for me outside my room. Just then, we hear a short rapping on the door, which sounds irritated. I instruct Alina to hide while I open the door. An imposing, but nevertheless short, agent. Probably five foot nine. Everybody is short compared to me. Except for Chromium.

"I am Krypton. Greetings Hydra."

"Greetings Krypton."

"Have you found any clues to her presence?"

Alina flinches. He notices.

"What is that?" Pointing to her hiding place, which, quite obviously, is not very good.

"This is... umm... My new servant. She is terrified of you. Most cowardly. Rise, *servant.*"

"Yes?" She says, rising slowly and timidly.

"Isn't that the Gold Princess of Allaara?"

"Depends on whether you want to maintain your employment or not."

Apparently, that is a horrifying prospect, because he promptly shuts up. I ask him to leave, and report again in the morning at seven fifteen. 'What did I do?' I wonder ponderously. So, I read up on Serpentin law, which needless to say contains far too much death and destruction. Alina is soon asleep, and I am alone with my thoughts once more. Serpentin law states subordinates must be kept in their place by the Hydra, and have the same laws applied to them as slaves. Which means... that threatening to remove Krypton from his post is the same as if a slave proved dissatisfactory. I may have just threatened to kill my agent. Not the best introduction. However, amongst all the gruelling and sometimes gruesome laws, I did find some items of value. Little did I know that later that night, I would have to use all of the knowledge I had...

I awake abruptly at two o'clock. Bolting upright, I know that something is wrong. Alina is nowhere to be found. A premonition, a terrible feeling… I must act swiftly. I pull on my black leather effect outfit hurriedly, and sweep my hair into a ponytail. Up. The lift is not fast enough. Finding the stairs, I rush up to the fourth floor. Nada is here. This is not good at all. Racing silently along the corridor, with only my Illumaen heart pounding incessantly. 'Supress the urge to panic,' I plead with my adrenal glands, which are already haywire. Krypton is there. Guarding the door.

"Let me in please," I demand, icily.

"I warn you; your servant has stepped too far out of line."

He opens the door and allows me entry. I hear Alina screaming silently. The fear permeates the air. Nada has her pinned against a wall, growling threats at her:

"You are going to suffer so much. You won't be able to scream. Nobody will hear you. You will be burnt, crushed and suffocated all at the same time. There is no escape."

I decide that this is a good time to interrupt her long speech.

"Hi."

"What, loser?"

"Incorrect. You may address me as Hydra."

"Oh, Hydra? Apologies. I haven't eaten in a while. I was preparing for a meal."

"Not anymore."

Alina at this stage is unsure as to look relieved or still terrified.

"You took my servant so you could eat something? Excuse me, but she's mine." I hate claiming ownership of other hominoids.

"Yes. After all, she is the Gold Princess of the Allaaraen Kingdom - what better way to force submission than to perform a manifestation of brutality and power?"

"Not under my government."

"What on earth has possessed you? We must further the empire's territory to achieve our utopia of monopoly."

"Have you ever considered a peace treaty?"

"That is not our way. Anyway, you were interrupting me. With all due respect, Hydra, I cannot wait to feel this worthless princess writhing in my stomach..."

She picks Alina up by the throat and lifts her over her head. Dangling her precariously above her mouth, which is now wide open (Serpentins can dislocate their jaw), she laughs sadistically.

"Article 15, paragraph 48, Section b."

"Shut up, you are ruining my digestion." Her jaw clicks back into place with a nauseating crack.

"This states that taking the Hydra's servant as your own is equivalent to high treason, and results in rejection or death. I do not think that you will cope very well with life on Americium (Americium is one of the moons orbiting Serpentin). Put her down!" I command authoritatively.

"Fine," she sighs sulkily, putting Alina down.

"Thank you."

"But... I need to see you walk out that door with a considerably distended abdomen, do I make myself clear? Or else you will be subject to acting against the interests of the empire, *Hydra.*"

"Accepted. Will you leave for a moment? I dislike being watched while I eat."

"Yes. I will wait outside with Krypton."

Alina is shaking violently in the corner, completely traumatised by her ordeal. I approach her and she embraces me, clinging desperately to my slim waist.

"Thank you so much for saving me, thank you Jade."

"You're very welcome, but it isn't over yet. I have to find a way for you to escape without Nada noticing."

"You can't. Nada can probably tell whether you ate me or not. There is no other way."

"You're right, I must…"

Chromium's warning rings in my ears as I struggle to come to terms with my task. 'No, I have to do this. I have no choice,' I tell myself with reluctant conviction.

"I understand. Is there anything I can do to assist you?" Alina slams the brakes on my racing train of thought.

"Well… this probably sounds impossible, but… try not to squirm or fight. I am not going to tell you that it will not hurt. However, not squirming around is possibly the best thing you can do to ensure your survival. Serpentin digestion is initiated by movement." At least I learnt something from those textbooks.

"Ok. I'm ready," she flashes a brave smile as she ties her hair back into a bun and slips her shoes off.

"Can you lie down please? I don't know how to do this."
"Sure…" Alina sprawls out on the end of the bed. She seems rather too relaxed, pretty much carefree despite what she is facing.

Exposing my abdomen so as not to ruin my t shirt, I pull her feet until they just about dangle over the edge. "I'm sorry," I say my last words to her, and she nods. I dislocate my jaw, which is extraordinarily painful, and takes a few attempts before I force it out of place with both hands. I have never done this before, which is quite an excellent thing. 'I certainly will not do this again' I determine with conviction. 'Well, I guess that sooner is better than later,' I think as I let her bare feet enter my oesophagus. They are cold, which I should have anticipated. I try not to bite her, but it is a challenge when I have had no practice in this awful procedure. I feel like I could suffocate, as I can't really breathe. This is absolute torture, both for me and her. Her shoulders are difficult to swallow, and I struggle greatly. Alina is visibly in pain, tears beginning to trickle silently down her cheeks. Empathy wracks my body. Now is really not the time for Illumaen nature to interfere. Eventually, the crown of her head slips into my mouth and down into my stomach. My centre of gravity is shot, and I bend double with the extra weight. Strangely, though I resist it, it feels quite fulfilling to have such a large meal in my digestive tract. I surmise that this particular feeling is quintessentially Serpentin. She didn't taste that bad either, a little salty I suppose. That could have been her tears though.

Regaining my vestibular capabilities, I take my hand off the desk I had used for balance, and as leverage to rise from my knees. Now able to walk, I cautiously open the door to the hotel room. I smile smugly at Nada and Krypton, and state; "I can assure you; this princess is not going to be in existence for long."
With that, I walk unsteadily down the stairs to my room, which is on the second floor. Entering my room, I simply want to collapse, exhausted. It is going to be sheer agony to regurgitate her. It would be so much easier just to digest her… but no. I am Jade Firedancer - an Illumaen first, Serpentin second. I will do anything to protect the lives of innocent people. I sit on my bed, steadying myself for my next ordeal.
   "You are doing great Alina. I'll get you out pretty soon. I need to know where your parents are first though."
Suddenly, an object is pressed against my pyloric valve. Initially, I surmise that it is simply discomfort from having such a toll on my stomach muscles. But no, this seems to be purposeful. I promptly cough it up. It is Alina's communicator. Quickly, I press the button, and immediately Sara answers.

   "Hello darling, are you ok?"
   "Hello Queen Sara. This is Jade. I need you to meet me somewhere so that I can give Alina back and we can negotiate a treaty between our peoples. Please come quickly… her time is running out."
   "Of course. We will have landed in an hour."
   "Ok. Follow my directions to get to where I am staying in Warsaw…"
I rapidly explain our location, before shutting off the transmitter. Short of breath, I place my hand gently on the top of my extremely strained stomach. Apparently doing this is meant to sooth an unborn child, but I

really cannot fathom if that tactic is going to work at this present moment. Stroking my abdomen, only very gently, my stomach muscles lurch. The feeling makes me want to wrap my arms around my midsection. As soon as I act, I recall my folly. I am now a living time bomb - Serpentin digestive acid is twenty times more potent than a human's. Bracing myself and steeling my nerves, I begin to wretch...

After half an hour, my consciousness fades. Unfathomably worn. I awaken gradually, to Alina staring into my eyes. I freak out entirely, almost screaming with terror. "Sssh," she croons, taking my right hand.

"One thing that is remarkable about you Serpentins, is that your muscles simply snap back to their previous position, despite being stretched drastically," she comments, observing my exhausted torso.

"Oh, Alina, you are remarkable. You yourself have been through intense torture, and yet you still focus on the positive. You are an exemplary optimist."

"That is debatable. Once I heard a joke about an optimist and a pessimist - the pessimist says; "This situation cannot get any worse." But then the optimist pipes up, saying; "Oh yes it can!""

This for some unknown reason makes me laugh so much my stomach hurts - although at this point it probably doesn't take much for my stomach to hurt. It must have been some phenomenon for Sara to knock at the door, hearing us shrieking with laughter. Making myself presentable, I answer the door with Alina standing directly beside me.

"By the way, Alina seems to have appointed herself my sidekick." I smile in jest.

"I thought that her time was running out."

"Yes, it still is, but it will take an era to explain the circumstances."

I take a deep breath, and give a synopsis of what occurred that night. Alina helpfully interjects numerous times in order to personalise the events, once more her relatively carefree, bubbly self. Unfortunately, this results in Queen Sara being transformed into a pale, *Zachwyt Kviat* hue. As dawn approaches at five thirty a.m., Sara and Alina leave, peace treaty in hand, hand in hand. How sweet and pleasant the mother-child relationship is when in action!

I sleep until six thirty, when I am awakened by a rapping on the door. Carefully and softly opening it, I am immensely surprised. Instead of Nada and Krypton glaringly studying me, Chromium is standing there.

"I thought that you were coming later on."

"No, I saw that Krypton and Nada had left, so I decided to come."

"What? When? Why? How?"

"Well, at least you have now exhausted all possibilities of questions."

"That was a humorous observation."

"Really? I do not ever recall anybody ever commenting on my sense of humour."

"Interesting. Anyway, back to my queries. Firstly, how did you know?"

"The Illumaens keep tabs on all civilised planets which are not involved in interstellar warfare."

"Ok. Good to know. I can also find this out?"

"Yes, all you need to do is contact communications using your earpiece. I have an earpiece, although a self-made one."

"Thank you. I ought to prepare for departure, I think that I will return to Illuma for a short period of time."

"Excellent! I can then commence teaching you the piano."

"That would be most beneficial. I am going to change into my jeans, so could you leave please?"

"I watch you while you are sleeping..."

"O... kay..."

"Joking."

"Good."

He leaves and I quickly ready myself for the long journey ahead. By the time I am ready, Chromium has remotely brought my *Jet Bubble* to the airspace above us, landing using his mind. "Another of my inventions," he comments. It is almost infuriating, but at the same time charming, how intelligent and yet how sweet Chromium is. Soon we board the *Jet Bubble* and head for Illuma. I am somewhat saddened to leave Poland, but a new adventure awaits wherever I go it seems.

Scythaon, Illumaen, and a Maelstrom of Other Disputes

Landing outside the council building of Illuma, Chromium and I part ways.

"I must go back to my laboratory; I have some things to attend to."

"I am going to brief the council regarding the developments in the Scytharian regime."

"Ok. Farewell."

"Au revoir."

I have no idea why I just bid goodbye in French, but Chromium responds:

"Au revoir ma meilleure amie."

"Le même," I smile back.

Likewise, my friend. Although, in my opinion, it takes a little longer than three days to call somebody your best friend.

Inside the huge hall, the council has already gathered, owing to our swift telepathic communicative abilities. My father stands in the most authoritative position, greeting me with a stately nod. I am most inappropriately dressed for the occasion, wearing jeans - this I am reminded of when I glance down the table where the members of the society are seated. All Illumaens are required to wear black and white suits for the meetings of the council. Thankfully, it seems that all is forgiven, as nobody bats an eyelid as I sit down at the table, at the head closest to the exit.

"Are there any matters requiring discussion?"

I stand and announce:

"Unfortunately, the Scytharians are planning an act of war against the Illumaen Union. They may try to enlist the help of the Serpentin Empire, which is essentially a totalitarian state, with my subordinate Nada playing dictator. I have very little control."

"Thank you. We are currently informing all in the Union concerning this."

With that, the meeting is over, with no further discussion. I immediately make my way to my assigned quarters (all Illumaens are assigned a home according to their requirements). I am just about to change from my jeans into my suit when a sonic boom echoes overhead. 'Scytharians,' I surmise. The second bang is a bomb, which lands perilously close to my quarters. Grabbing a light brown leather jacket, I flee in the direction of the science quarter. While it is relatively hot on Illuma during the day, at 300 degrees Kelvin, it becomes bitterly cold at night, sometimes dropping below 273K. My current attire should stave off hypothermia and heatstroke, with a white t-shirt to reflect the starlight, light blue jeans, light brown boots to shield my feet from dust and freezing temperatures, and of course my jacket. Leather effect material is the most practical in this situation.

I hurl myself through the door of Chromium's lab just as another detonation ruptures the path behind me. Panting, I stand up. Chromium is also standing, readied for a refugee situation. He is holding two items: one is a magnetosphere creator, and the other, a pendant of gold. Set in the middle of its striking gold surrounding, is a Jade stone. It hangs tentatively on the fine chain, polished and precisely cut into a teardrop shape. The stone itself is a rich green, mottled with flecks of red, highly polished. The gold surrounding is fashioned into intricate gold leaf, with four leaves on each side and two supporting the stone at the bottom.
    "Take this," he explains, handing me the pendant.
    "Are you sure? This stone is highly valuable."
    "Yes. I just made it. It will complement your eyes and your hair. I wished to convey my friendship."
    "I cannot express my intensive gratitude in words."
Chromium tremors a little.
    "Words are not required. I felt it."
Turning around and pulling my hair aside, I ask that he put it around my neck. Shaking a little, he fastens it by its clasp. Smiling softly, I face him.
    "It looks beautiful on you," he whispers. Gazing into my eyes for a moment, he eventually explains his soul-stare: "Your eyes are like deep

water, sparkling on the surface, but nobody really knows what hides behind those glittering eyes."

"I thought that we could read each other's minds."

"Not necessarily. We can only transmit what we want to convey. Otherwise, where would the magic of friendship be?"

"That is true. What a glorious poet you are."

"Thank you..." his voice trails off as we stand together in surreal silence for a moment.

The heavenly silence is promptly shattered by the din, not of a bomb, but of an unmistakeably Scytharian fighter, flying low overhead. "The back entrance!" Chromium shouts, and we dart out into the open. "Look, there are caves over there. Will we be safe there?"

"Yes, they are deep. I studied those caves' topography when I was ten."

"Do you think that they will look for us?"

"Most likely. I am the top scientist, and you are the Ambassador. We represent a large amount of power."

"Knowing something about Scytharian terror tactics would be useful..."

"I know a little, I'll inform you later. But now, we MUST get to those caves before the rebels catch us."

Dashing swiftly along the dusty road, avoiding the shrapnel from the bomb, we come to the bottom of a steep path. Sure footed as ibex, we leap through the loose rocks, above a vast valley which stretches into a dry riverbed. Finding a small cave, I beckon Chromium to come with me. But he has eyes on a much preferable prize: a highly elevated position, almost inaccessible. 'We'll never get up there,' I think wistfully. 'We can Jade' - Chromium has heard my doubt.
With that, he begins to climb, tying his black fleece around his waist and hauling himself onto a substantial boulder. Doing the same with my jacket, I take his outstretched arm and scramble onto the first rock. A fall

would be certainly fatal. The only way is up. Fortunately, my boots are sturdy and support my feet well as I struggle up the rock face.

Closer than ever to our prize, muscles aching with exertion. Slipping, slipping. Precipitously, unhindered, fail to grasp. Breath escapes my lungs, caught painfully in my throat. Suddenly, a hand, a saviour, pulls me to safety. We both collapse majestically in the sun, finally atop the ledge. It's 296K out here, and Chromium is panting alarmingly.

Stumbling to my feet, I take one last look at the Illuma I know now - it will never be the same again. The only constant in life is change: the shifting of the dunes, the growth and withering of plants, birth and death, weather patterns; ever changing, ever transforming. Such is the nature of life. Gathering my energies, I help Chromium into the shade of the cave, as dry as the surface of Venus. Still, it is our only respite. So begin the hard times, the life of a fugitive. The sun sets, with the orbit of our fifth moon interfering with its rays, reflecting a metallic and shimmering sphere onto the council building. Folklore has it that this is why the great hall of the council was built there: to be bathed in the halo of the moonlight. Tomorrow is a new day, a new challenge, a new chapter. I shut my weary eyes, astounded at the magnitude of the universe, and the folly that is war.

Lone Sentries in the Desert

Morning rushes into the cave, shedding blinding light on our gently tanned skin. I rise, shaking the dust from my hair and sweeping it into a neat bun. Chromium is laid out rather serenely, and yet I see the dehydration telling on his visage. It is beginning to warm once more, now about 288K, and rising fast. I must find water before the sun sears the sand and rock. "Higher, Faster, Stronger," the Olympics motto resonates in my mind. The higher I go, the more likely the morning dew is to condense into small pools. There is a lip of rock above the cave mouth, and the smell of water is welcoming, and yet torturous. I leap to reach the ledge, catching the rock and my muscles tensing to hold me up. Swinging my legs to the side, friction being the only force that holds my feet to the sandstone. Performing a dangerous gymnastic feat, I bridge my body and reach with my right hand towards the tiny droplets of moisture. Cupping my hand, I carefully collect the water, sipping gratefully from the cool condensed vapour. The next handful I use to wash my face, before I trust my judgement and let go. My boots impact the ground with a thud, which awakens Chromium with a start. He rouses tiredly, and breathes:

"Water…"
"I have found some on top of the cave mouth. You must climb to reach it."
He produces a tiny measuring spoon, with the capacity only for a tablespoon at most.
"Please get some for me. I have pulled a muscle in one of my arms."
"Ok, will you be alright?"
"I should be."
With that I recommence my pilgrimage up to the pool of dew, collecting the water in the tablespoon and handing it to Chromium, who drinks it enthusiastically. After about five runs, I use my left hand to scoop up water, and splash his face. The cold water revives him a little more, and I jump back down to the edge of the cliff.

"There is a castle on a cloud…" I commence singing a song I memorised while on earth. It reminds me of my childhood, when everything was so much simpler. My voice causes Chromium to stir, and genuine delight radiates from his eyes. I never knew that eyes could be so expressive.

"Your voice is like the celestial repertoire of a choir of angels," he interjects, freely expressing emotion for the first time to me.

"Thank you. What a pleasant and eloquent compliment."

"You're welcome."

I gaze out over the horizon, where smoke shrouds the land like war, and the scent of terror permeates these mountains, the pervasive air of suffering from the Illumaens down below running for their lives. A glimmer of light from the surface, a silver vestige of reflected rays. 'A scout for the rebels,' I ponder. Abruptly, the light moves.

"They have seen us Chromium," I gasp. "They can bomb us out of here if they want. We must get down from here."

I begin to search for an escape route.

"I forgot to tell you; they are going to torture us for information regarding the Illumaen Union. I know about their defence systems, and you have the security clearance necessary to hack into their computer systems."

"Now really is not the time to focus on our impending doom. We have to get off this ledge."

"We could jump… that lower ledge is not more than seven feet below us."

"Yes, but what if either of us slips and falls?"

"The sand should provide sufficient friction to arrest our descent."

"Ok. Let's do this."

With that, I steady my gait and step off the cliff. Terrifying weightlessness ensues, the air tugging at my arms and legs like strings. Then, as rapidly as I fall, I land successfully on my feet. My knees bend as I absorb the impact with my hands hitting the ground just after my feet. Straightening up, I signal to Chromium that he is cleared to jump down. He lands in much the same manner, crouching like a cat ready to spring at any moving object. As it happens, we were not a moment too soon. A huge crack resonates as the rock buckles under the pressure of fighter fire, which drills holes in the rock and undermines the ledge we were just standing on. Like meerkats, alert and sharp, we shimmy down to the next ledge. The valley gapes hungrily at us as we balance on the edge of its mouth.

As the popping of the ammunition draws closer, our plight develops an uneasy urgency. Flight is a much-required gift, often overlooked by mortals. The stones are slippery and loose, and we slide dangerously down the slope. The expression "to hit the ground running" illuminates my neural network. We will both hit the ground facedown if we run any faster. Momentum building, adrenaline rising. 'Wherefore shall we fly should we be greeted by angry men?' my mind races. Surely, my intuition is ominous. Wrenching ourselves around a corner at an unsuitable velocity, we are greeted by a band of rebels. They stand stolidly at the bottom of the slope, poised with their guns loaded and ready to kill. Scytharian soldiers are indoctrinated to believe that the cause of the empire is more important than their own life. Not dissimilar to the Serpentin military concepts. That is why they often join forces to create an undefeatable alliance. That is what the Union is so afraid of.

"Come with us, you worthless idiots. Did you really think that you could get away with this? We are exceptional at torturing those whom have information. What a prize, the scientist and the diplomat at once!"
"We will not go down without a fight," I snarl at the commander.
"Oh yes, you are…" he smirks as two of the soldiers shoot darts between our eyes. A dizzying sensation, then vacuous darkness.

I awaken gradually, first only aware of sounds. The whirring of machines operating, the harsh clanging of metal, the shrieks of horror-wracked beings. Then sensation returns, the cold, damp hardness of the floor on my back as I stir, and a throbbing pain in my head from the stun gun used to knock me unconscious. Next sight, although there is little to look at. Only a monochromatic, grey cell. All of the same grey material, like concrete. It is rough, only adding to the sense of impending doom. Sitting up, I face the only change from the matte-grey surroundings: Metallic grey bars which lock me away from the outside world. Where is Chromium? He must be nearby. He is in great pain; I can sense it...

Bolts being unbolted, voices in the monotonous whirring. Clinking as a rotund prison guard strolls past. The keys on his belt create a quiet drumming, the beat of slavery. Two heavily armoured soldiers march noisily up to my cell, possibly for dramatic effect. "Come with us, *Illumaen,*" they snigger. It is not the correct time to divulge my identity. Fortune comes to those who wait... They grab me roughly, handcuffing me and pushing me towards the now open door.

"Your friend is very stubborn - he will not talk."

"Well, Illumaens have a gift for robust pain thresholds."

"Yes, and loyalty too."

"An obvious conclusion."

Walking proudly down the corridor, they unexpectedly shove me into a room. Chromium is there. Tied to a chair using steel restraints. They swiftly do the same with me, opposite him.

"Now, boy, will you talk to save your partner in crime?"

"I will never talk." There is blood streaming from his mouth.

"Fine then. I have here a bottle of hydrochloric acid. It is so potent; it will burn all the way from your mouth to your stomach. You will die."

"How can you be so sure? You don't know how strong my oesophageal lining is." I reply somewhat defiantly.

"We know how Illumaen digestion operates. You are not equipped to survive this. Chromium, you still have a chance to save her..."
I smile slyly at Chromium, who returns the communication.
"Never."

With that one of the guards forces my mouth open while the other tips the whole litre of acid into my mouth. By the end I have successfully bitten one of the guards, drawing blood, and snapped the neck off the bottle. Being half-Serpentin has its advantages. Perchance you now think this book is going to end tragically. I am going to die. You cannot kill the protagonist and then continue the book, can you?

Well, fortunately Serpentins are not affected by acid, which is why I didn't die after swallowing Alina. Their oesophagus is lined with a particular form of cell which is resistant even to Serpentin stomach acid. The guards stand back and admire their failed handiwork. One of them is whimpering in the corner, due to their incised finger. Some macho interrogators these are.
"Well, that didn't work," one of them mutters.
"Seeing as you seem callous to chemical assault, perhaps a little asphyxiation is in order."
"You shan't get any information from me."
"We need the clearance code."
"Thank you for stating that."
"Bring out the board."

There is a technique known as 'waterboarding,' which results in the victim feeling like they are drowning, or otherwise dying. So, this is what they are going to attempt: psychological torture which affects even the strongest of minds. They abruptly pull me out of my restraints, which have left marks on my wrists, and presumably my ankles. The slam is muffled by the black soundproofed walls of the circular room. My back twinges as they restrain me to the board with thin metal handcuffs. Already my mind is anxious - how much of this can I take? I push away my anxieties, and consider instead the events of the day. Aching all over from exertion and survival instinct. A black cloth smothers my face, and my claustrophobic breathing is tiring me. The water will come in a moment. My throat clamps up, as if I am choking. Unexpectedly, and still predictably, the slightly viscous liquid cascades onto my face. I cannot see it, but psychological agony is felt rather than seen. 'Remain calm and rational,' Chromium's thought advises me. What is rationality? What is this that I should not die instantaneously? The water will asphyxiate me at any moment. My lungs gasp for air, and I hiccup with fear.

"Do you want me to stop?"
"Not if it means surrender."
"Oh, we have a feisty one here. It might take a little more to break her spirit."
They cease pouring water onto me, and leave me, still restrained, on the board. I hear them exit the room, although I am disorientated.
"Jade, are you still sane?"
"I think so. Is that you, Chromium?"
"Yes, it is I."
"That was quite arduous. I can tell why it is ordinarily so effective."
"Thankfully they do not possess Veritas serum. It breaks even the highest IQs and the most determined and secretive minds."
"I have not heard of this before."
"It is a chemical I made and tested a year ago. I immediately destroyed it, so that only I know how to formulate it."
"That is a relief."

The interrogators march purposefully back into the room (it seems that you can decipher much from sound alone) and remove the cloth over my face. Finding your prisoner smiling at you must be a first for them, as they start when they see my facial expression.
"Why are you smiling?"
"Because that is the only way to defy you in this situation - to be exultant despite torture."

"Well, you just ran out of luck - there are some extremely convicted Serpentins here who cannot wait to get their teeth into you. Send them in."

I draw a controlled breath as they strut in, as if they were peacocks trying to attract a mate. 'Well, I don't think these Serpentins would last very long on their home planet,' I consider gleefully.

"Hello useless *Illumaen*," the leading interrogator crows.

"We like the taste of flesh and blood. I'm sure that you'd rather give up the information than be our next trophy."

"Perhaps you underestimate me. You have no idea who I am. Who sent you?"

"We are supposed to ask the questions," he whispers huskily in my ear, running his hand down my arm conceitedly. "But, seeing as you asked so nicely... the head of intelligence on Serpentin, Hans is his name I believe, gave the order."

"I see."

"Now, we have given you information, how about a little gratitude, brat."

"Or else?"

"Or else... we have a skillset in eating people."

"That doesn't scare me."

"Really?"

He leans in so close to me that I can smell the vengeance on his breath. His anger. Irrational and burning anger.

"But a bag over the males' head." His assistant obeys immediately, albeit with an air of nervousness. And I thought that we had free will... I guess that we lose everything in the name of conflict and jubilation.

He firmly places his outstretched hand on my stomach. "I bet you have stunning musculature," he whispers.

"Yes, I do actually. Get off of me."

"Only... if you give me that clearance code."

"Never."

His hand is moving slowly down. If I wasn't restrained, he'd be quite affirmatively unconscious. My t-shirt is in minor disarray, revealing my toned abdominal muscles.

"Wow - I certainly wasn't expecting abs that good."

"I can assure you, if I could use them right now, you'd be the size of a hydrogen atom."

"Ooh, we have a Serpentin mind here. What else did you unearth in your meaningless studies of us?" he teases intolerably.

"An awful lot. You would not be doing this if you knew who I really am."

"How peculiar. So, I suppose that I wouldn't do this either?"

He swoops in and kisses me all too forcefully. I struggle against my bonds, and he only becomes more enthusiastic. Biting is an option, but is unfortunately an expression of affection in Serpentin culture. I utter a silent wish: 'please let him see my earpiece, then he will know.' But no, alas. I flinch as he bites my neck with vehemence. 'I have to get his attention somehow.' My Illumaen mind courses with options and consequences. A decision must be made rapidly. I reach my conclusion, and the scientific method is reversed; the conclusion enacted before the hypothesis or the experiment. Using all of the willpower I have left; I wait for his next assault on my lips. This time he has gone too far, and though Serpentins have no gag reflex, I am half-Illumaen. I gather my thoughts, and return his "favour." He is helplessly locked in, unable to pull away. He finally notices my earpiece. I wonder how many non-Serpentins he has interrogated like this. Stunned and taken aback, he steps away and simply stares at me. I am panting slightly, but that just adds to the dramatic effect.

"Are you… Hydra?"

"I am indeed, and I believe that what you just did was an assault on your Empress," I snap.

"Oh no, no, no… you have to let her go, let her go…" he stammers, before falling to his knees, gazing nervously at my stomach.

"You weren't serious about the strength of your muscles, right?"
I have never seen such fearful and hopeful eyes in a man.

"You were following orders. Now, go back to Hans, and tell him that he is going to answer to Hydra for his treason. Go!"
Needless to say, he scurries off hurriedly, with his minion in tow.

Rising, I release Chromium from his bonds, rearranging my attire and wiping the taste of bitterness out of my mouth.

"Come on, we must go to Serpentin," I speak softly. He lifts his bodyweight, and stumbles.

"Are you alright Jade?" he coughs weakly.

"Yes, I am still in one piece. You, however, do not seem so high spirited."

"No, they gave me acid before they brought you in. I have lost vast volumes of blood. I will not survive much longer."
I carry him outside, where the war seems so far off, and red-stained cumulus clouds hang on the horizon. The sky is a deep orange, and the sun dips slowly behind the mountains all around us. I sit and lay him out on the sand, cradling his head in my lap. He is breathing too quietly to sustain his blood.

"Take care of yourself Jade," he whispers hoarsely.

"No, you will not die Chromium, no, you can't go..."

"Leave me here - save yourself, please."

"I cannot leave you, I will not..."

"I am tired, so tired... tired." He closes his eyes softly.

"Sleep well, for you will awake once more."

"No... this is my final sleep. You have shown me life, how to live. This is my final farewell."
He reaches up to touch my face, and my tears dampen his cold fingers. He grasps my pendant, and utters a single phrase:

"Jade... I love you..."

"Chromium, I love you as if you were my brother. I would give my life for you. Please don't go..."

"No, it's not like that…"

With that, he gathers all of his meagre strength, and pulls my head down. Our lips make gentle contact, before he falls back onto the ground, cold and weak. Surprised and stricken with a sudden flood of grief, I put my head on his, listening to his breathing as it fades, slows, shallower still. It stops like the chiming of a quiet bell, serene and resonating, the last striking of a tuning fork… then graduated silence. His heartbeat decreases in poignant increments, before I can no longer detect a pulse.
"Leave me…" his words echo in my skull, and press painfully on my chest. I must get off planet. But I do not want to abandon him…

A decision - I will honour his wishes to take care of myself, though my heart is breaking. Clutching my necklace, I rise and walk sombrely in the direction of what is left of civilisation. There will be a Serpentin craft I can take to Serpentin. The soldiers will let me in, especially since Hans' servants fled through here. By dawn I board a *Jet Bubble,* and progress sadly to Serpentin. A fire burns in my heart, a sensation of retribution - but no. Revenge gets one nowhere. The Illumaen must suffer in glorious silence, the revelation of emotions is irrational in this situation. If I lose it with this leader, he will probably die. I don't want blood on my hands. Still, I must confront the one who murdered Chromium. I vow to lock my personal feelings in a vault until further notice. Calm washes me clean as I turn the key and toss it into the depths of my mind. Now I truly understand why Illumaens are so efficient. They leave emotion out of the equation entirely. But is it an advantage to them, or a curse? I am certain to discover the answer at some point…

Hans and other Petulant Leaders

I reach the military base on Serpentin in rather a stately manner. The dome directly behind my palace is not a disadvantageous location for the centre for military intelligence in this practically totalitarian state. Dumping my luggage regally (although I am unsure as to how one does that), I prepare myself to essentially rant epically to Hans. I wonder, which style of clothing would be most intimidating? It appears that in my absence, the little seamstress has gone quite mad, creating a multitude of tops, dresses, and trousers. Such a remarkable woman. I must inform her of my appreciation. Unfortunately, Serpentin fashion is not exactly in my taste: all of the tops are too short. At least the climate here is fairly mild all year around.

I stride into the main building wearing white jeans with a silver button, and silver zip pockets. My white top has flowing short sleeves, and cascades down my back to my waist. I debate as to whether to hug a book or something to conceal my exposed abdomen; it is very uncomfortable to have various Serpentins staring at your centre of gravity. The neck of the top is embroidered in geometric silver lines, all parallel, progressing around my neck in a diagonal fashion. My clavicles are softly illuminated in the yellow light of the chandeliers above my head. For all intents and purposes, the look of serenity and tranquillity.

Entering the room in which Hans and I have arranged to meet, he is already seated on a red and gold embroidered sofa, not dissimilar to the pattern on the ones in my quarters. Again, it is awkward when the first recognition you receive is a glance at your navel. He is sitting in a dominant posture, filling the seat confidently. He directs me to sit opposite him.

"Greetings most exalted Hydra. What ushers you here?"

"I think you know why I am here. You did not consult with me before destroying my people and my planet."

"It was a beneficiary strategy for the empire. The Scytharians have long been our allies, and we now have a renewed supply of servants."

"I would like to be consulted before any military action is enacted in the future, do I make myself clear?"

"The law states…" he leans forward, his hands forming a steeple as he rests his elbows on his thighs. Ha! It would take a little more than that to intimidate me.

"The law states that any assault on Hydra, her family, or possessions of value is punishable by death!" I finish his sentence, probably slightly differently to how he would have. "You sent your minions to extract information from me and Chromium. I have severely reprimanded the investigator, but you carry the weightier sentence."

"Umm… well… you certainly know the laws of Serpentin well. We will incorporate your new wishes," he stutters slightly, no longer dominant, rather, submissive. Now I guess is a good time to assert my authority.

Rising, I place my feet in front of one another slowly and in a stately fashion, stepping around the glass table between us. Standing squarely in front of him, I glare condescendingly down at him.

"Now, remind me what the execution form for treason is…" my voice drips with sass.
He looks up imploringly at me, and gets no response. Bending at the waist, I lean to whisper in his ear. He flinches upon feeling my warm breath on his earlobe.

"I think you know what comes next."

"Y-y-yes."

"Excellent. That means that you do have some form of common sense in your cranium."
As I straighten my back, I notice his eyes tracking from my mouth to my stomach.

"Get up!" I bark. He starts, before doing as he is told. Standing to the side, I signal for the servants to leave the room.

"Come over here." I only hope I haven't gone too far. He is shaking in much the same way as Alina was - it must be a common psychological tick before one is swallowed.

Standing face to face with him, I participate in a brief staring match with him before he breaks the stare. He makes the fatal mistake of looking back again. Slowly reaching my right hand around his throat, I lift him with apparent ease. To tell you the truth, this exercise requires a substantial amount of effort. Dislocating my jaw, easier this time, I tip my head back slightly. He makes no attempt to resist. He obviously knows that opposite action is futile. Silence slices the room like a dagger. The only sound is Hans struggling to draw breath...

The following morning, I awaken with a wonderful feeling of contentment. At last the planet is in equilibrium once more. I now have control over the military, and have both the commanding officer and Nada wrapped around my little finger, so to speak. Glancing down at my flat stomach, I smile. 'No need to threaten any longer,' I consider. Sitting up, I switch my earpiece on. Nada is asking me to come to a meeting regarding breaking our alliance with the Scytharians. "Excellent, all is arranged as planned," I commend her.

I arrive at the meeting dressed in a red suit, with a grey top and shoes to complement it. Trajod is sat at the other head of the rectangular table, as per usual glaring at me. Evidently, he is incredulous that I am both Serpentin and Illumaen. He is small-minded. Speaking of small-minded, to my left sit three of my captains and admirals, along with Trajod's servant Alpha. Beta, Nada, Hans, and a Scytharian admiral sit to my right. Hans looks most unimpressed to be seated directly beside me, and scowls in a bizarre manner at me.

"Now, Ambassador Trajod, we meet once more."
"Greetings Hydra."

"The motion we will be discussing today is the severing of our military alliance."

"We have served your empire well," the Scytharian general interjects.

"Yes, and our appreciation is conveyed. However, an amendment must be made to the treaty between the two empires."

"What might that be?" queries Trajod, as per usual, sarcastically.

"We cannot continue to assist you in the defeat of the Illumaen Union. It is illogical in a political sense for Serpentin to contribute."

"Are you sure this is not personal?" One of my own is taking a dig at me. I rectify the situation by smiling disarmingly at him.

"My personal feelings do not factor. The empire is much better off conquering other systems, rather than sharing custody of a few planets."

"Speaking freely, the Scytharians would rather have full custody of the Union," Trajod admits proudly.

"We have already withdrawn our troops, thanks to Hans' excellent organisational skills," Nada shoots sarcastically at me.

Hans nods, glancing at me and touching his neck, possibly without realising. Perchance his hands are cold. However, that is not likely - it is a reasonable temperature of 297K in here.

"So essentially you brought us here to inform us that you are refusing to help in the control of the Illumaen Union. We will most certainly lose against the Illumaen defence strategies. Did you at least get the codes?"

"No," Hans contributes rather feebly. "We tried to interrogate the chief scientist, but he died before he could give us the codes. You will have to find your own witnesses to interrogate. Illumaens are fiercely loyal."

"Fine. We will. Good day, and don't expect this to end here, *Hydra*."

"Good day Trajod. Have a pleasant trip back to Scythaon."

After the meeting, Nada sees fit to "educate" me in the life of the average Serpentin by taking me through the streets at night. I decline, so instead she assigns Hans to show me around. He just stares wide-eyed at

Nada, before hesitantly agreeing. I think that perhaps Nada enjoys the pain of others. This conclusion must be concealed, or I may next be at her mercy. Even empresses can be irked.

We arrange to meet at the Platz at 1700 hours (Serpentins have a twenty-hour day). I don my high waist blue jeans and a striking navy top, which falls softly to my hips and is delicately decorated with gold square gems, which adorn the edges of the garment. Hans opts for an almost gothic look, wearing black jeans and a charcoal grey fleece. "Do you have any idea of where we are going?" I inquire.
"Wherever the mood takes us," he replies cryptically. Well, at least he seems not to be so afraid of me any longer.

The streets are painted a stormy grey by the dark cobble stones paving the streets in neat rectangles, and by the dull buildings of the common people, in contrast with the bright political buildings. As we walk down the main street, the sheer hedonism of this species is evident in everything around us. My Illumaen sensibilities are pricked somewhat by all the decadence roaming the streets: lavish bars and nightclubs line the streets, and on every corner lurks someone ready to snatch a partner for the evening. Hans appears nervous. He moves in closer, his shoulder very nearly touching mine.

"This alley we are about to walk down is the darkest in this city," he explains. "Stay close, it is not safe for any lost Serpentin or otherwise." Evidently Hans is quite comfortable jeopardising my life again. How unfortunate.

"This is where slaves are traded. They are treated like animals, and really this is what Nada wanted you to see. She certainly wouldn't have described it as I have - she is one of the primary dealers."

How bad can the judicial system of this empire get? Blatant corruption goes unpunished and servants and prisoners of war are bartered literally as animals for the slaughter. Yet, I still see something in Hans... he is different. He has a certain empathy uncommon in a Serpentin.

The squalor and cacophony are worse than that of a slum on earth. Hans takes my hand uncertainly. Slaves plead with us as we walk past, and merchants display their wares on steel chains. My heart wrenches as a small girl cries in a corner, having been bought by a menacing looking man.

"Why did you bring me here?" I ask, utterly horrified.

"Nada ordered me to."

"Why did you listen to her?"

"She has connections in the hit industry."

"The what?! This just gets worse by the second."

"Yes, the Serpentins have the equivalent of the Mafia. Officials who rebel simply disappear one day, and it is usually Nada who is smirking at their memorial."

"Could I reform the system?"

"Perhaps - but no. They transcend common status boundaries. A couple of generations ago, a Hydra tried to instigate reform… but they simply vanished one day."

"So, in other words, it is futile to resist the flow of this society."

"Yes. There is only quiet rebellion, under the radar, so to speak."

"I see what you are indicating."

"What do you think?"

"I think that he is a fine specimen," I comment.

We have paused in front of a man, not more than twenty. A low ridge dividing his face down the middle until the end of his nose, and his striking black hair with streaks of dark brown, indicate that he is Oplexus. I finally discovered that the Oplexus are a race who the Empire conquered approximately thirty Serpentin years ago. I can still see the fire of resistance in his eyes, a steeled determination to defy his captors. Money exchanges hands, and on a tight chain, I exit the alley with the trade of a highly corrupt official.

"That should be sufficient to fool Nada."

"Hopefully."

We return to my quarters at 19:30. Inviting him to sit, Hans and I have a glass of what is similar in taste to tea, but is the hue of blood. Hans tells me the name of this odd drink, but I soon forget what I do not deem important.

"What I want to know is, why do Serpentins execute people by eating them alive?" I ask Hans.

"Well, it is kind of complicated. You see, it has everything to do with control. Sometimes the only way to get people to fear you is to confront them with something unknown and terrifying."

"The great unknown is the first thing that we are afraid of as children."

"Precisely."

"That makes a certain amount of sense. But why not kill them first, if that is the reason?"

"Questions, questions... There is also the concept of torture. Someone like Nada, who is experienced, can keep someone alive for forty-eight hours before killing them. Until then, they are trapped, and gradually digested by gastric enzymes, which burns like nothing else in this Galaxy, as you can imagine. Worse still are the stomach walls, which are so strong you could break someone's bones by squeezing," he gestures towards my stomach.

This is the oddest conversation I have ever had with someone. I am trying my absolute best not to appear completely weirded out...

"Surely it hurts a Serpentin to do that though. I mean - to have someone squirming inside you for two days."

"Most of us find it sublime. We are unusual in that our brains release serotonin and dopamine when we feel them fighting for their lives. I know that Nada finds it entirely delicious."

"How many people have you eaten in your time?"

"I think only one, at my Initiation ceremony. Every male has to eat a person upon reaching eighteen, like a transition to adulthood. But males do not often eat people. They have no real need to, and usually they are the ones who get eaten, by their partners."

"There is a bit of a black widow relationship then, among Serpentins."

"Sort of, although servants are the exception, for the reasons I gave earlier. Mostly it is only the women who eat people regularly. Their metabolism is faster, and they need the nutrition to support their fertility."

"O...kay? I kind of get it, but don't??"

"Yeah, women are weird."

"Certainly Serpentin women are anyhow," I muse under my breath.

"So, what happened to Kasia, the Silver Princess of Allaara?" Evidently, this is a question exchange system. Unless Hans could just be attempting to change the subject, not so subtly.

"What about her? Silent rebellion is all we have, is it not?"

"You did not kill her?"

"No."

"This Illumaen heart of yours is going to kill you one day. Be careful who you trust Hydra."

"Call me Jade."

"Jade."

Dismissing Hans, I change and clamber into bed. Exhausted, I shut my eyes to the cruel world outside. It seems, that when one is born, though we see in colour, everything is black and white. Gradually, ever so gradually, it fades around the edges, greying as the hair of a human. Then a rift grows between black and white - insidious grey brushstrokes on the flawlessly divided canvas. Soon, it shall be difficult to distinguish the black from the white. My mind fades to darkness, worn down from the enigmatic tangle of lies that they call an empire.

Desolate Democratic Dealings

I awaken abruptly and most cruelly. I had been in the most utopian dream. I am standing outside the council building on Illuma, the dust whipping around my face, tousling my hair with it. Then I see him. Chromium. Running towards me. We embrace, and I breathe his warm comfort. His gentle hand touches my cheek. A moment that could last forever. Alas, this is not to be eternal. No utopia ever is.

I come to rather suddenly, distraught and more exhausted than when I fell asleep. Emotional agony does strange things to you sometimes. My servant is hovering anxiously around me, eager to please. Pulling together an outfit, I alight at the door to what is technically a kitchen. He beams at me and asks:

"Is there anything you need, exalted one?"

"First, perhaps you can tell me your name?"

"My father always used to say that you should never name an animal you are to eat."

"Yes, that is a beneficiary principle, however I do not wish to eat you."

"Oh - well, I have been conditioned for three months on how best to act when dealing with ones' master, so I suppose that I am simply reiterating my training. Nada teaches the hostages twice a week."

"Wait, you guys get lessons?!"

"Yes."

"This is an appalling state of affairs. I must do something..."

"Do not even think about trying. Our society struggled against the Empire and its ways, and see how far this valiant rebellion got us," he gestures towards his humble attire.

"I will see you when I return, but for now I must go."

He seems almost pitifully desperate. Still, he seems genuine, and exceptionally well-mannered. If he weren't my servant, I would employ him as a respected member of society. Serpentin has such a twisted view of other races and species. They believe that they have a right to kill, simply because they are "better." They are not "better," maybe nobody is truly "better" than anybody else. Existence seems to me like the great leveller. We are all gifted in some way, and our downfall will invariably be someone else's gift.

All of a sudden, I remember how much needs to be done this morning. I leave quickly, despite not eating breakfast. I'll have time later, I guess. I have various errands to run today, although it seems a relatively quiet day compared to previous days. Just a triple check that the military isn't bombing anything without my permission... Then, I see it.

A piano.

A striking black, polished body, with excellent quality keys. A distraction from my schedule, but not an unwelcome one. Mesmerised, I approach it and sit at the leather-covered stool, running my fingers up and down the smooth, lustrous keys. A masterpiece. I press a note. Only middle C, but a ringing beauty captivates me. Gradually, I find a tune. Only Für Elise, only the right hand, but an immersive blanket of sound which soothes my soul. Suddenly, salt in my wounds, burning pain, unquantifiable sorrow. I am reminded of Chromium. I see his face. He is wearing an expression of inexplicable melancholy, an encompassing look of despair and hope. Bowing my head, a tear rolls down my cheek and onto B flat. My chest feels like it is imploding, and my diaphragm heaves as I try to contain the pain I had locked away for too long. It rises as a darkness, powerful and uncontainable. I stand up with difficulty, and turn. Nada is waiting for me.

"Greetings Hydra."
"Greetings Nada." I struggle to sound relatively normal.
"I heard from Hans that you purchased a servant."
"Yes, at his advisory." Still shaking, my chest heaves as I suck in air to calm myself.
"Indeed. Hans is an excellent advisor." She is glaring piercingly at me.
"Is there something else?"

"Yes. I have obtained information that you did not in fact eat the Silver Princess of Allaara. Explain yourself."

"It was not necessary to kill another hominoid. A peace treaty is far more rational than fighting a war against the Allaaraens."

"You speak like an Illumaen!" She hollers deafeningly at me. "You fail to understand the true meaning of what it is to be Serpentin. You must eat and digest the servant you purchased, and you will not be permitted anything else until you do."

"Since when were you higher than I am Nada?" I counter aggressively.

"Since I became the *Tradition Keeper* of Serpentin. The law states that the *Tradition Keeper* has the obligation to prompt a Hydra to act in the interests of the Empire. You must learn to become more Serpentin. Why, you even went and made a peace treaty with those Allaaraens; Now we have to give the remaining hostages back."

"A challenge you have presented to me, and I shall rise to the occasion. I will not eat. You are dismissed Nada."

I no longer am sufficiently inspired to play the piano; it seems that this planet crushes the very core of a rational being, a compassionate being, and twists it into darkness and hate. I only hope that I will not undergo this devastating fate. Once more I lock my emotions away and swallow the key with my salty tears. With nothing more to do, I saunter ponderously, sombrely, back to my quarters. Hans is strategically placed at my doorway, grinning all too smugly.

"You told her about Kasia, facetious viper!"

"May I point out that viper is a compliment on Serpentin. I had to..."

"Why?"

"In order to prolong my life."

"That is as good a reason as any. Who threatened you?"

"Nada. I have the instinct that she would quite like to eat me."

"Is that an idiom, or should it be assumed as literal."

"Serpentins, unlike Illumaens, speak literally rather than in pointless idiom."

"Understood. Good day to you, as you are a stranger to me."

"Goodbye."

With my shoulders back and chin up, I stride into my quarters with a backward glance at Nada, who is currently stalking me rather obviously. She thinks that she is discreet, but truly she isn't. I have seen the way she eyes Hans. 'Don't worry, I will certainly not deprive you of your infatuation,' I direct the thought towards Nada. If only she were Illumaen...

"Greetings Hydra."

"Greetings..." a staged pause prompts him to speak.

"Widner. My name is Widner."

"Pronounced like a "V" or a "W"?"

"V."

"Right, Widner. Things just went pear-shaped."

"I am confused."

"I am half-Illumaen, remember?"

"Ah, yes, comprehended."

"You seem quite well educated."

"I taught myself to read, I found some books in the shell of the education centre on Oplexus. Well, that was before I was found and taken here."

"Most remarkable. How did you find the time?"

"The Serpentins destroyed our infrastructure first, and then took us while we were weakened."

"I still fail to understand this system present on Serpentin. It makes essentially no sense to me."

"You speak like an Illumaen - eloquent."

"Thank you. Nevertheless, there is an enormous issue to explain. May we sit...?"

Widner seems quite lucid to my predicament, but maintains that I should simply do what Nada says. They live in morbid fear, these servants. A waste of intelligence. I can only see through Illumaen eyes, a frustrating ideology at this stage.

Illuma. That is the solution. Leaping to my feet, I announce my imminent departure. Nada decides that Widner and I need chaperoning, so launches Hans into the situation. He is less than impressed, to say the least. Although, on reflection, fear for one's life tends to overrule petty differences. Widner glares at him suspiciously as he climbs into the *Jet Bubble*.

"Widner, this is Hans. He is the advisor who suggested I consume you." Widner shoots a look of death at Hans, who appears physically hurt.

"Stop fighting children, or you'll both end up dead," I smile sweetly. Promptly, they both bite their tongues and sit back in their seats. As we take off from the small landing pad on the outskirts of the city of Serpentin, I consider it an ideal moment to highlight the submissive qualities of Hans.

"Nada has you tied to a post like a horse, Hans."

"I know. In the beginning I actually believed that she could love me. I wanted to marry her."

"We have a marriage institution on Serpentin?"

"Yes, but it is seldom used. Most males are eaten before they get a chance to even think about it, and the females... well, they are self-explanatory."

"Almost every custom and practice on Serpentin is an aberration to my sensibilities," I sigh.

"Many newcomers discover that to be so."

"I am unsure as to whether Nada is capable of the love required for marriage."

"I unearthed that too late. She has me tangled in her web of deceit and lies. It is only a matter of time before she kills me."

"I am still amazed that there is absolutely nothing I can do to reform the debauched society of Serpentin."

"No, there is nothing anyone can do," Widner and Hans speak in chorus.

As we exit the atmosphere, I cast my eyes back to the surface. The two poles are yellow with frozen sulphur ingrained in the ice, and below the two poles, lush forests thrive. A melee of different shades of green. From here a couple of lakes and rivers split the trees, on one side flowing and on the other frozen over like glass. The main city sprawls across the lush landscape like a huge spider, with roads leading to smaller settlements among the greenery. A beautiful planet, marred only by the urban jungle spanning a quarter of its surface. I kick the main engines into gear, and set a course for Illuma. Goodness knows what I may find when I get there…

The Game of Chess and The Game that is Life

I land the *Jet Bubble* on a recently renovated landing pad on Illuma, about 300 metres from the council building. My father comes out to greet me, glowing with discreet delight at catching sight of my visage. This elation is fleeting, extinguished by the sight of Hans and Widner. Ushering our small troupe inside, he invites me to come and play chess with him. Widner and Hans are quickly volunteered to help with the recovery work in the area's roundabout. "They are both strong, most notably Widner - he is Oplexus," I explain. The work overseer looks quizzically at Widner; he has likely never seen a dark-skinned member of the Oplexus race. I barely noticed, given my upbringing on earth.

"Excellent, we are just recovering the rubble of the hospital and science labs, we could use an extra two brains," he gets over Widner's appearance, switching back to Illumaen logic.

Noticeably, Illumaens replace the role of the hands with the brain. My father gestures for me to sit at the white side of the gleaming chessboard, highly polished marble with exquisitely carved pieces.

"I really think that I ought to be seated on the black side. After all, I am half-Serpentin."

"If you are referring to the dystopian values that Serpentin upholds, then you are comparing a game of chess to our lives."

"Correct."

"I was hoping that we would have this conversation."

"I also find it pleasing to elaborate upon the analogy of chess."

"Chess represents the hierarchy of life. Some, like you, are a Queen or a King. Others, like Widner, are likened to the pawns, carried about by the whim of their superiors."

"Agreed."

"Nevertheless, the chess game of life is far more complex. Sometimes a pawn can become a Queen, and a King a pawn, a bishop a knight, a knight a castle."

"Hans used to be as a knight, strong and with an upper hand. But now, he is but a pawn, leashed by another who craves control."

"Yes, indeed. Such is the human factor in a game of chess."

"So, if one wishes to extend the analogy to real life, one would have to transfer the board and pieces into sixteen-dimensional space, where they amalgamate and separate and oscillate simultaneously."

"Yes, exactly the point I was representing. One can learn much from a simple game of chess..."

"Check," I move one of the knights.

He moves a pawn to defend his king. I move my queen in an attempt to checkmate him.

"Checkmate." He has moved a castle.

"Well, that was rather a rapid game."

"We Illumaens pride ourselves on our speed at calculating possible repercussions during chess sessions. We all play chess daily to sharpen our mental faculties."

"I find my intelligence a disadvantage at times. Do the rest of the members of the council experience this?"

"Oh, yes, of course. Some people, other species, have their senses dulled so as not to cut themselves on reality. An Illumaen must learn from infancy to wield their weapon of intelligence with skill, for it only takes one blow to maim a situation. Such is the fatal drawback of our enlightened senses and minds."

"This statement is an excellent description of the plight of those with high IQs," I muse ponderously.

Instantaneously, an entourage of hominoids with hooves rather than feet trot in.

"Greetings, Illumaen council. I surmise that you are engaged in the riveting activity of chess."

"Indeed, we are. I am Jade, the Ambassador. To what do I owe this pleasure?"

'This is the Promethean delegation,' my father silently informs me. 'They care for half of the Union. We shepherd the other half. They are related to us in intellectual capacity, although they are slightly more eccentric than us.'

'Thank you for the update.'

"I believe I have not met a Promethean as of yet," I continue my introductions.

"Greetings, Jade. We have heard much regarding you and your intellectual achievements. Our condolences regarding Chromium, his inventions prevented the Scytharians from taking our sector of the galaxy."

"Yes, he was a remarkable intellectual..."

"We were considering kidnapping you and testing your intellect, but we concluded that that would not be beneficiary."

"May I convey my appreciation that you decided not to kidnap me."

"It would have been amusing."

"Quite." They certainly are a little more eccentric.

Suddenly, a work overseer rushes in with Widner in tow:

"We have just found the last theory Chromium worked on before he died - it is revolutionary!"

'Don't allow your emotions to get in the way,' I command myself sternly. I then take charge of the situation, exclaiming;

"What is the purpose of it?"

"It is a dimensional jump theory, based on the hypothesis of simulation particles. It means that if we correctly programme our craft, we can leap in and out of this dimension, dissipating and reappearing at will, like a simulation particle."

"What a wonderful theory!" One of the Prometheans bursts out excitedly.

"What did he term it?" I ask curiously.

"Strangely, he usually gives his theories numbers and codes, but to this one he gave a name: The Firedancer Theory."

"How intriguing."

"In my opinion, the name should remain The Firedancer Theory, for it describes the theory aptly," another of the delegation chips in.

"He named a theory after me?" I query tentatively.

"It appears so, Jade," my father muses ponderously.

The momentary silence is broken by one of the Prometheans, who rushes over to my father with the greeting:

"How fare you Lawrence? I have not seen you for at least a year by the Illumaen calendar (eleven months)."

I thoroughly agree that they are extremely eccentric. Still, at least presently I know my father's name. 'Lawrence. So, this is the name you so stubbornly refused to present me with, Father?'

'I was attempting to illustrate a point.'

'I received this communication almost immediately. Illumaens do not rely on simple names. You make a name for yourselves through your reputations.'

'Exactly. Your first lesson in Illumaen culture.'

"Let us drink tea and eat cake," a member of the delegation pipes up.

"Apologies, I have extensively studied the human condition," they explain.

"I understand. However, I am in no position to eat cake. I am on hunger strike."

"For how long?"

"Until Nada dies."

"Well, that is not going to happen any time soon, I can assure you," Hans interjects, as per usual, irritatingly.

"Nevertheless, tea is prepared for all who wish to partake," my father offers to ease the swelling tensions.

As we walk into the room to the left of the Great Hall of the Council, one of the Prometheans requests to sit beside me.

"I have a great interest in literature, particularly Shakespearean works," Cordelia assures me. "I and my sister Regan, who unfortunately was not selected for the delegation. It is the work of my family line, studying the literature of other cultures. My other sister parted with the tradition, becoming an analyst, but is also highly successful. We have found humans to be the most engaging - all regarding the same themes, yet different in each subtle and unique manner. Nuance is highly prized on earth, is it not?"

"I concur with your well-informed hypothesis," I answer as we are seated with a view over a plateau to the west of the building, the opposite direction to the mountains where Chromium and I once fled.

It seems, that for every meeting or otherwise activity I participate in on Illuma, there is always someone or something which abruptly and inconveniently interrupts. This time it is a dark figure, which I spot lurking outside the window. All black attire, and a nimble but strong build. Her face is covered, except for her eyes. She appears engrossed in staying out of sight, although quite blatantly failing. I suppose that it depends on who she wishes to hide from. Silent and benign, however threatening. Cordelia is engrossed with explaining her findings regarding the anthropology of King Lear, so I am safe with my paranoia. I look back, and she has vanished.

Suddenly, I am informed of some new guests to go and greet outside. I acknowledge a few of the Illumaens returning from Serpentin captivity, (I was able to pull a few strings so to speak) as I walk past the landing pad. Thereafter, strolling casually, but with correct poise and purpose, I spy the six-person entourage awaiting my presence. The tallest, a man with dark brown hair and electric blue eyes looks protectively around. I instantly recognise his family; an attractive woman with shoulder-length brown hair, and their two daughters. Two servants, one a gentle young woman in her twenties with kind grey eyes, and a handsome blond man, flank them in an effort to secure them. The oldest girl squeals upon catching sight of me, and runs rather enthusiastically towards me, garnering a defensive crossing of arms from me.

"Jade, Jade, you're here!" Alina shrieks at a soprano range, hugging me. These Allaaraens really are fond of hugging and other forms of contact. Sara greets me with a kiss on each cheek, Darius the father shakes my hand, and Kasia beams up at me as if I was the saviour of the galaxy.

"You rescued my sister, thank you," she smiles quietly.

"Never mind that the rescue was unpleasant," Alina jokes.

"Yes, indeed," I chuckle slightly. "Welcome to Illuma. What brings you here?" I query.

"We have come here to formally seek asylum for our people until our infrastructure is repaired," Darius speaks authoritatively.

"Well, currently we are in the process of re-creating our own infrastructure, however we will endeavour to accommodate you until such a time as you can return to your home planet."

"Our gratitude cannot ever be conveyed."

I notice Kasia staring vacantly towards the council building, transfixed by some thought or object.

"Are you ok?" I ask sensitively.

"I miss Proximus..." she drifts back into her reverie.

"You will see him again; I am sure of it. In your heart, deep down, you know that he will wait for you."

Meanwhile, Alina is having an avid discussion with Widner; goodness knows what about. He doesn't seem nearly as eager to talk as her. Scanning the surroundings, I observe the workers painstakingly removing rubble and clearing the sites where new houses will be built. Illumaens are highly efficient, and thus they use the materials from the ruins as mortar and other materials to build the new dwellings.

There they are again. The mysterious hominoid in black is pressed up against a building, watching the proceedings. A terrorist? Unlikely, there is little to be achieved by attempting an attack on Illuma; the residents are far too rational to view them as a threat. Certainly, they appear to be analysing me. I beckon for them to come closer, and they vanish, melting into the surroundings as a shadow with the light. The soft promise of an iron threat casts a shadow of illumination over me.

Back to Serpentin, a Crèche for Idiots

As the light of the Illumaen star changes wavelength from a composite to 650 nanometres, and the light diffracted from the atmosphere stains the horizon red, Nada shrieks once more down my earpiece. One simply cannot glean a moment of respite when trying to prevent several conflicts at once. It is a highly arduous profession, politics. I exhort that none of you ever achieve a rank in these dealings on purpose.

She, of course, wants me back on Serpentin so that she can keep an eye on me, although this is not the reason given, that being that she wishes Hans to be in her presence. Simultaneously, news is transmitted from Allaara, and so Alina and Kasia travel with me to visit briefly. I cannot comprehend why they enjoy my company; I was almost responsible for both of their deaths. C'est la vie. Landing skilfully in the North Meadow, I scarcely open the pod before the girls are battling to be first to step out. The blue grass has taken on a tranquil scent, freshly trodden by a herd of unicorns.

"They sleep in those caves over there," Kasia indicates some magnificent crystalline structures marking the North Pole. A chill pervades the air, quite unlike the warmth I experienced coming here the first time. I suppose that this is the furthest point from Rigel, the star. Suddenly, a glimpse, a fleeting memory of joy. Alina beams elatedly as Dach gallops enthusiastically towards her. I turn my head for a moment, and she is there. The omen of a force, the eyes of a spy. Dark brown eyes regard me, and I regard them, before I turn my back on the piercing daggers and re-focus on the reunion occurring before me.

Kasia squeals with unbridled excitement as Proximus whinnies, thundering delightedly towards her.

"I thought I'd never see you again!" She cries, embracing his strong polished neck.

"I am sanguine to gaze upon you once more," Proximus nickers into her wind-ruffled hair. Even Daisy makes an appearance, cantering up to me and nuzzling my cheek with her silvery muzzle. I gently run my fingers through her silver-white mane a few times, before turning to go.

"I must go, Serpentin requires my supervision. I am saddened to leave you, but be assured that I wish to visit sometime in the near future. Farewell my friends."

"Farewell!" They utter in harmonious chorus, before Alina steps forward.

"Here, take this," she offers a *Zachwyt Kviat* to me.

"Thank you enormously," I curl the corners of my lips maternally at the small band of bystanders. "I shall wear it in my hair I think." I push it in between the silken threads on the right side.

"So long, and stay safe!" we all shout to each other in unison as I close the pod and fire up the *Jet Bubble*.

Hans and Widner join me at the main city of Allaara, the buildings broken and the fountains dry from fire. Stones are scattered brazenly across the streets, but still the children play around them. Restoration is already underway, re-carving the ancient designs and hauling great foundation stones to re-build the devastated homes wantonly shattered like Grecian vases. I see Sara and Darius helping to direct the work, their spacecraft parked in the meadow nearby, poised for when they must tear themselves away once more and fly to Illuma for refuge. The people have a remarkable ability to hope, to regenerate, to clear away the sharp rubble of the past and construct an entirely bright, carefree future upon the remnants of the old. That is perhaps the greatest quality I admire of the Allaaraens; their shining promise of something better, a durable delicacy which surpasses any other civilisation I have observed. I push my tears back, swallowing the lump in my throat as we take off, heading for the darkness of Serpentin.

My stomach breaks the paradisiac peace in the craft, snarling at me in protest. I have not eaten in three Serpentin days, which is typically how long us Serpentins can go without a fresh meal. I apologise for my impertinent outburst, getting a smooth reassurance from Hans. Widner, meanwhile, curls up in a corner, trying to make himself as small as possible.

"I wouldn't do that Widner," I laugh playfully, "Curling up into a ball is not the ideal modicum of perturbing a ravenous Serpentin."

"Yes, of course Hydra," he straightens up, his back rigid against the seat. After several hours of unbroken silence, we reach Serpentin. Hans exits first, beaming beatifically at Nada, who is impatiently tapping her left hip, with an intolerably smug expression on her defined features. I step out next, with Widner last, scurrying around me in an attempt to appease.

Hans bids farewell to me, with the words;

"You are the most pleasant Serpentin I have ever met. I am afraid that I may not see you again," his eyes flicker towards Nada, who is poised with hands on hips, running her tongue across her top lip. "Stay safe. Serpentin is a cut-throat society, literally."

"Farewell Hans. You are a… good person," I smile ruefully, unable to formulate any more eloquent adjectives. Gazing after him, I track his movements as he strolls into the distance, grasping Nada around the waist with his right hand as they round a corner. She reacts by swinging her head towards him, staring ravenously into his eyes. Hans may be correct; I am not likely to see him again.

Widner interrupts me;

"There is someone here to see you, a woman… I think."

It is her. The enigma, the apparition who has stalked me throughout my trip. With still only her divisive eyes glaring out, her speech is muffled ever so slightly by her mask.

"I am a servant, trained specifically by Nada. She commanded me to ensure that you did not consume anything other than your servant during the course of your trip. You succeeded."

"Thank you for informing me of your somewhat devious intentions. May I ask your name?"

"Nada said that you are not to know my name. K, you will know me as."

"And so you remain a mystery…"

"Can I just say," she blurts quickly, "That you have a moral strength uncommon on Serpentin. I applaud you. I must go…"

"Farewell, and gratitude," my expression softens into a warm glow.

In actual fact, I feel rather light-headed. Performing my daily rounds of the intelligence centre, I point out a few anomalies, before trudging exhaustedly to my quarters. Widner offers me a little herbal tea, hailing from his home planet, but I decline. Nothing will supress the hunger rising inside me. He fusses around, trying to make me comfortable, but at this stage everything I see is potential nutrition. My digestive system complains again, startling Widner.

"I think you should leave, Widner. I know you are jumpy, and this state of affairs is not exactly going to improve," I giggle a little, looking at my abdomen.

"No, I will not rest until we can solve this conundrum," he replies firmly, plonking himself down on the sofa opposite my chaise lounge. Sighing, I turn away from him, my arms crossed as if to contain my impulse to eat. Sleep takes me by the hand, leading me into restless, ceaseless dreaming.

Awakening with a start, I am greeted by a very tired Widner, who is still waving tea under my nose.

"Wakey, rise and shine Hydra!" He has a cheesy grin plastered on his face.

"Morning Widner," I sigh tiredly. There really is nothing more to be said. Dressing, I prepare myself for another long day trying to keep tabs on interstellar chaos. My stomach aches for sustenance, but I ignore it to further the cause of my hunger strike. I never particularly understood why people participate in hunger strikes on earth; however, I finally comprehend their reasoning. They are fighting for what they believe is just, not unlike me refusing to take the life of another creature. Sweeping my hair into a half-ponytail using an ornate silver hair fastening, I adjust my black jacket and set off.

First, to the intelligence centre to examine our copious supply of weaponry, and to ensure none have vanished. All is present and correct, although the staff are indescribably bored with my lack of enthusiasm to blow things up. Well, that's what you get when you deal with a half-Illumaen. In fact, since Serpentin stopped wantonly destroying cultures, there has been a seventy percent decrease in rebellions against the empire. An era of peace has begun, an era of creeping, stealthy reform which will hopefully take the illegal underbelly of the planet by surprise. I only hope I live long enough to see it without being assassinated. Hans' words remind me that I am taking my very life into my hands, stopping the wars. At times I simply cannot fathom this people - they are irrational at times, and I cannot abide irrationality.

I request a ledger of the staff; all are present and correct. Well, that is, aside from Nada and Hans. They have not reported for duty as of yet. Should I pay a visit to remind them of their duty to the empire? It would definitely give Nada a taste of her own medicine, despite my instinct that she has a wholly different taste in her mouth at present. I rap impatiently on the door, staring expectantly at the blockade, lest it open. Nada yells in a somewhat affected tone;

"Come in, I won't bite... just now." Pushing it open, I climb the three steps up to the living area. With some flourish, I open the inner door to find Nada sprawled sideways across her chaise lounge. Her lungs seem taxed with the effort of breath as the life squirming inside her taut stomach ebbs away.

"Hans?"

"You guessed correctly. He didn't struggle as much as I'd hoped... I much prefer it when they fight," she comments in a non-descript, compassionless manner, stroking her abdomen, and smiling psychopathically.

"You have such a sick mind."

"Oh, I'm not sick... I'm Serpentin. By the way, you have not eaten your servant yet. How disappointing."

My stomach selects this moment to growl venomously, causing even Nada to raise an eyebrow.

"You really should eat something."

"The earth expression of 'I could eat a horse' takes on an entire new meaning."

"I am going to escort you back to your quarters, where Widner is waiting patiently for you."

"Ugh..." I am defeated. Nada rises slowly, one hand planted on the top of her abdomen as her prey shifts in what I can imagine as intense agony. Life is so fragile, painted delicately on the edge of existence, so easily blotted out or crushed...

Sure enough, Nada has sent her servant before us to announce our approach to Widner, who is rooted to the floor as if he were a tree in the living room when we alight at the doorway. Weakly acknowledging him, I collapse onto the floor. Nada, wielding a dagger, instructs Widner to put me on my chaise lounge. Promptly, almost as soon as she arrives, she wanders back down the street to her quarters. Faint from lack of food, Widner seems blurred and everything in the room is drifting. Removing my jacket, he cautiously exposes my torso.

"What are you doing?" I query groggily, before he replies shortly:

"Nada told me to do this. She mentioned that it would force you to swallow me."

"No..." I whisper with the effort of refusal as he runs his finger up and down my torso. Swift at first, gradually slowing to a precision metronome, activating my gastric enzymes. I feel my stomach flooding with chemicals, and I shift uncomfortably in my desperate fight against myself. 'Do not start circling, no circles, please no,' I beg Widner silently as he changes tack with light circles along my muscle lines. The feeling is overwhelming, pleasant but torturous simultaneously.

"Too much, too much!" I shout in exasperation. "Come here, you good for nothing slave! Stand a little closer, yes you can feel my breath. Stay right there!" Switching from reclined to upright, I pick Widner up in the throes of an impulse. My jaw pops out of place and I practically ram him down my oesophagus. It is difficult to control something this heavy with one arm, so I support him at either side of his shoulders to avoid too much pressure on my stomach at once. As I discovered previously, the shoulders are the most pressing issue, however a few concentrated contractions make light work of this barricade. I close my eyes with pleasure as his head slides effortlessly down my gullet, before inclining my head to inspect my handiwork. I feel nauseous, but finally I have satisfied my over-demanding digestive system.

Collapsing back to a seated position, I take in a few deep breaths, partly to give oxygen to my lungs, partly to try and stop the meal in my stomach squirming so much. It is highly uncomfortable when your prey is thrashing about - you truly cannot think straight. Half horrified by my actions, half revelling in Serpentin emotion, I manage a flicker of a contented smile. Why, how indeed, did I come to this? My Illumaen half bellows ethical principles at me, while my Serpentin half screams that this is the right thing to do. After perhaps half an hour, my brain has worn itself out, from running in circles of ideology. Massaging my distended abdomen, I sink into an exhausted trance, slipping away into a deep slumber.

Awakening by minute degrees, I come around with a sense of confusion and a lack of knowledge as to what has happened. I regain consciousness mainly because Widner kicks my ribcage.

"Ow!" I jump, or at least try to jump.

"Aw, are you so weak that a kick injures you?" Nada is standing in the room, taunting me. Her tone is similar to that employed in speaking in mock sympathy.

"Flicking your abdominal muscles will crush them. Try it, it's fun."

Remind me not to take any further advice from Nada.

"He'll probably die of pain in a couple of hours, seeing as this is the first time you have digested someone. I am proud of the fact that I can keep my prey alive for up to forty-eight hours before finally crushing their bones..." she squeezes her fist to demonstrate.
I cannot help noticing that her abdomen no longer moves with the indication of sentience. Rolling my eyes, I ask:

"What is the time?"

"Oh, 9 o'clock or so."

"I'm late! I have to check on the uprising on Augustium, and make sure you lot haven't created a new bill of rights in my absence!" My Illumaen practicality hits me like a ton of bricks (Apologies for my ubiquitous simile).

"Whoa, you are not, going, anywhere!" Nada exclaims. "I have found you a new servant. They will take care of you and bring you the reports."

She brings out the new servant, a quiet girl of not more than nineteen in earth terms. Lanky and spindly, reminiscent of a sapling, with a shoulder length bush of red hair.

"I am from Xenon. I will be loyal to my death..." she stutters slightly. Her distinctive amber eyes reveal as much about her race. My stomach gurgles threateningly on cue, causing her eyes to widen in fear.

"Now, there we go, all sorted. I'm going to leave and attend to my duties. Remember that you are serving the Hydra, prisoner 68539." Nada thankfully leaves after that minor warning to the Xenonian.

"Thank goodness she's gone!" I startle the servant by speaking.

"I-I suppose that is what I ought to say..."

"It's ok, I don't want to scare you. We got off to a dismal beginning, Nada was never the gold standard in introductions. I am the Hydra, which is what you must call me in public, but otherwise you can call me Jade. I am half-Illumaen. What is your name?"

"I am Eimear. As I said, I am Xenonian. I somehow sensed that you were not entirely Serpentin. Serpentins are far more sadistic than you are."

"It is amusing that you can say that, in spite of my current situation..." I glance down at my bulging stomach.

"Indeed..." she muses thoughtfully. "This might sound strange, but can I ask you something?"

"Of course, Eimear."

She reacts positively to the sound of her name, as her eyes flicker in recognition, before she continues speaking:

"Does it hurt? I mean, to have such a weight in your abdominal region?"

"It does hurt, but Serpentins have very robust muscles, which is why Nada is able to crush her prey. This is the first time I have actually done this; it is bizarre." I shift a little on my perch, lying on my side.

"You don't strike me as a Serpentin who does this regularly..."

"No. Nada drove me to hunger strike in order to coax me."

Eimear laughs pleasantly, a sweet, uncaring laugh, almost fake, but genuine. I smile generously, due to the impossibility of laughing.

As if to arrest the refreshing moment, I get the sensation of severe pain in my stomach. The ceaseless movement which until now has dominated me is slowing. 'He's giving up,' I realise with a twinge of emotion.

"I'm sorry Widner," I murmur to myself, before mustering my strength. Euthanasia seems to be the fairest option in this instance. Breathing out forcefully, I pull my abdominal muscles in the direction of my spine. Shaking a little, the effort is an effective test of core strength. Eimear starts as a sickening crack announces death, and my smooth abdomen is moved no longer by the desperate writhing of a man in pain. Still struggling under the influence of weight, I move a little. A miscreant tear rolls down my face, and I decisively sweep it away.

Imprisoning my Illumaen emotions, I repeat over and over again in my head: 'You are Serpentin, you are Serpentin.' Exhaling slowly, I run my right hand tenderly over my still protruding torso. Eimear looks at me, and I at her. No word or recognition or emotion or regret betray my blank stare at nothing.

A Memorial, a Eulogy, a Resolution

As was prearranged, Chromium's memorial occurs one Illumaen month after his death (thirty-five days). Dark clouds loom over head, foreboding precipitation. A small crowd of us, the council and a smattering of scientists who survived the war, gather around his modest black headstone. Our heads solemnly bowed in respect, and, for me, grief. A brief summation of his life and works ensues, including his scientific, musical and linguistic feats. I blink back burning tears, and silently stare at my polished brown ankle boots. We dress in white for the occasion, and my cotton dress reaches to my mid-calf. Only a thin plaited brown belt breaks the colour of my attire, and the wet stains of my tears on my high round neckline. I stare into my gleaming necklace to focus my thoughts. All too rapidly, it comes time for me to speak. Shaking, I step up onto a small, polished podium of light brown wood, hailing from the most impressive of the Illumaen trees.

"We are here today to celebrate the life and mourn the loss of Chromium." I begin uncertainly. "You have all just listened to the definitive list of his marvellous achievements, and we all appreciate the fine, hard-working, honest, and compassionate young man he was when he died."

My voice shakes a little, so I take a deep breath before continuing:
"Selfless, he gave his life for the good of the union and for us. However, you have heard all of this previously. I would like to focus on what Chromium would like us to strive for, to continue doing. He stood for discovery, truth, knowledge, understanding and harmony. His very work preaches these things. He was a scientist and a musician. Remember, that every time you look up at the stars, you can see all the beauty, pleasure, pain, promise, potential, darkness and light in the Galaxy, and indeed the universe. Always remember this, that no matter how much you solve the mysteries of the universe, how much scientists rationalise every star, constellation and galaxy, there is always so much

more to be learned. Let science inspire awe and wonder, not make everything mechanical and dull."

More confident now, with my head held high, I conclude:

"This is what Chromium would like us to remember; remember the founding basis for our culture - the search for truth, justice and knowledge. Thank you."

With that, large droplets of silvery rain begin to fall on the parched, dusty earth, for the first time in seven months - the wet season has commenced.

Table of Contents – Part Two

Back to "Normality"

As I make my way back to the council building along with the others, Eimear tries to shield me from the unexpected downpour with her hands, apologising profusely as she fails spectacularly. I look back at the council members dismantling the podium and hurrying inside to protect it from the drops cascading from the sky. Rushing inside, I check and double check that my white dress hasn't suddenly become see-through from the wet. It hasn't thankfully, so I wipe the hair sticking to my face away and behind my ears, before stopping, just for a moment, to think. What is my next move? Which interstellar disaster do I have to avert next? I am genuinely surprised that the Scytharians didn't blow up our little memorial gathering. Eimear presents me with a beautifully soft sky-blue towel with silver leaf motifs with which to dry my face.

"Thank you," I barely smile. I have learned not to smile too much, at least not with those hailing from Serpentin. It scares the servants, because they think that you are plotting to kill them, and other Serpentins... don't smile. Unless they are thinking of eating someone. Then it's scary, especially if the smile is directed towards you.

To be honest, Illumaens cannot see the importance of smiling all the time. But they do, sometimes, when their emotions spill over into their facial expression. We have incredibly strong emotions and emotional states, but due to our telepathy we instinctively know how another feels before they even display it. It is a delight to see an Illumaen smile, as it is symbolic of the offering of their joy to you, the desire to share their happiness with you. With humans, they smile out of sympathy, or to make the best of a sad situation. Worse, they sometimes smile when they in actual fact don't really mean it. There is none of that superficial nonsense with Illumaens. They only smile if they have one extremely good reason to.

Brushing the excess moisture off of my jaw, I put the towel back in Eimear's hand. Turning, I am faced with a concerned Illumaen.

Telepathically, he asks; 'Are you okay? You were close to Chromium.' Unable to respond, choked up with emotion, I look up into his grey eyes, allowing a single tear to escape my right eye. It isn't only a smile that Illumaens rarely reveal. He responds in kind, his mouth twitching down at the corners briefly in a flicker of melancholy. He touches my shoulder firmly, before walking off behind me.

"He touched you," Eimear observes with shock.

"He is Illumaen. He is not bound by Serpentin tradition," I reassure her, and she falls silent, unconvinced. No one must touch the Hydra. She is too goddess-like to be defiled by the mortals she rules. She must give express permission before someone can approach her. Only a servant can have physical contact with her without permission being given. For example, Eimear is allowed to help me dress (although I do that myself), and to shield me from peril.

Switching my earpiece on, there is first a crackling, then the characteristic rhetoric of Nada demanding that I return to Serpentin. Poised to reply saying that I will be there very soon, my father walks up with a grave expression on his face.

"There is something of vital importance you must be informed of."

"Okay, I will be in the society hall presently," I acknowledge. "I may be a while Eimear. Feel free to sit, or mingle, or do something, in my absence."

"Why would I do any of those things? My only purpose is to serve you, and then provide you with nourishment when you wish, when you tire of me."

"Just... Relax then. Don't worry about me or anything else. I did eat this morning!"

"Okay. I will try," she bows her head, retreating to the nearest seat: a long bench up against the grey-brown polished wall opposite the door to the society hall. I shake my head disapprovingly as she sits stiffly, bolt upright and legs crossed awkwardly, hogging the left arm, made of finely crafted steel.

Opening the door to the hall, I sit at the head of the table, only having to stride a few paces before reaching my seat. I look up and down the long rectangle, and the society members gathered around it on three sides, waiting for a sign of the meeting beginning. All of a sudden, my father clears his throat, and all turn expectantly to face him. Everyone is required to look at the leader to demonstrate attention - this is why the side of the table closest to him is empty, so nobody has their back turned during the convention. There are four either side of Lawrence, mostly security. They have some say in proceedings, but they mainly explain military and planetary security concerns.

"You have all been brought here regarding an urgent matter. You are all well aware of how the Illumaen Union operates, otherwise you would not be here. Ambassador, we are particularly reliant on your negotiation skills to re-balance this delicate and finely-tuned institution."

"What is out of balance, may I ask?" I speak out of turn, before being promptly put back in my box by a stern look.

"One of the planets under our care wants to break away from us. Become an independent entity. The Electrolans."

A collective gasp echoes around the chamber, so I wrack my brains as to what or who exactly these Electrolans are. Finding the profile tucked away in the back of my mind, I read it. They are an incredibly advanced and savvy race, highly intuitive. They are so finely tuned, they can harness the electrical current produced by all living things, most of all themselves. Like some eels and fish can produce electricity on Earth, the Electrolans can produce electricity. Now I understand why it is so important that they stay in the Union.

"Of course, each of you is also aware of the system of shared resources we have within the Union," Lawrence continues, prompting me to focus on the task at hand. "We provide the intellect and diplomacy to coordinate the efforts of all in this Union. The Prometheans assist us in this cardinal role, and there is a delegation with us today to aid proceedings," he says, gesturing towards the small crescent of

Prometheans seated directly below him, facing the table we are sitting at. They wave over-enthusiastically at us, betraying their bizarre eagerness for anything they encounter. Mercifully, there are only five of them, and 16 of us, including Lawrence.

"The Electrolans are our primary source of electricity. It enables the Union to sustain power without damaging the environment," an environmental scientist from our delegation stands and states.

"If they leave the Union, we will have to pay for their services. That would be disastrous. We only have enough resources to share, we did not factor in paying a greedy planet," a Promethean economist announces melodramatically, striking the desk in front of him with a crash as he hurriedly stands up. The Illumaens collectively roll their eyes without performing the physical action, sighing silently to one another.

Suddenly, an urge seizes me, and I stand up abruptly, startling everyone. I thought that I only unnerved people on Serpentin when I moved. Evidently that jolting presence has transferred to Illuma too. I must get that in check...

"What if the Electrolans are not greedy? What if they want a fair price for their work? Perhaps they want to build trade routes to other sectors, and return with things we as a Union cannot produce? At the moment only Illumaens and Prometheans have the right to trade outside the Union. Is that reasonable?"

I surprise even myself with my forward attitude. I am very much afraid that my status on Serpentin has gone to my head, and my individual opinions are affecting my ambassadorial work on Illuma. Even on Serpentin I am often told I cannot change things, much to my irritation. Nada, you see, is the *Tradition Keeper* of the Empire - she has to make sure that nothing very dramatic changes during the rule of the Hydra. It is most frustrating, that I cannot stop the slave trade, or the conquering of planets, or the pointless and inefficient destruction of resources on worlds we could make a deal with and have a mutually beneficial relationship with. The Serpentins truly know nothing of diplomacy. If I rock the boat, so to speak, I risk assassination. My subjects are obviously perfectly happy with their unethical ways and deeply flawed society.

After a moment's stunned silence, my father replies measuredly, but still indicating his disapproval.

"We must think the worst, and then we shall never be disappointed. In fact, this leads seamlessly into my next proposal. Jade, you are our Ambassador, and therefore the Ambassador representing the Union. Your next assignment is to go and negotiate with the Electrolans. Preferably, you are to dissuade them from leaving the Union. If not, form a deal which is fair and reasonable. We still need electricity, and the Electrolans still need some of our resources."

"You did not answer the Ambassador's question…" The person seated to my left stands up to stake a claim in the meeting, to the dismay of Lawrence, and the Prometheans. Clearly, they were hoping for a clear-cut and brief convention.

"That question has previously been considered, and our conclusion is immovable. We are the most intelligent, therefore we earn the right to control trade. Otherwise, our less intelligent allies might create dubious trade connections. We transfer our findings to all in the Union, so they are not left in the dark in these matters," the head of the Promethean delegation snaps. So emotionally volatile, for such an intelligent race. My secret supporter sits sheepishly back in their seat, looking at their reflection in the desk.

"Society convention adjourned," Lawrence quickly interjects, allowing the highly combustible atmosphere in the room to cool a little. I rise, making my way towards the door, when my father grabs my arm just hard enough so that I stop and turn around.

"Please, don't mess this up. The Illumaen Union is fragile. You must stop them from gaining independence."

"I will go and meet them now. I defused the Scytharian problem effectively, I can handle a trade dispute," I counter confidently. I find that simply listening is the key to good diplomacy. Listen, and then validate ·

the other parties' concerns before offering your point of view. Something I failed to do just before when speaking.

"I hope that you are correct..." he shakes my hand by way of farewell, before walking out with the Promethean delegation. They surround him like worried sheep, gesticulating and trotting quite loudly on the shining black floor.

Strolling to where Eimear is seated on the bench, I find her asleep, or rather, dozing. I don't think that you could ever sleep properly after being subjected to the training given to slaves on Serpentin. I brush my hand across her shoulder, and she awakens with a start.

"I was not slacking from my duty!" she pleads up at me.

"I know, it's okay."

She relaxes a little after my assurance.

"How was the meeting?"

"I have to go to Electrolaia. Diplomatic affairs call."

"Right... Nada is going to eat you when you get back if you do that..."

"Who cares? If she touches me, I can eat her. Then you will be spared for at least another week," I grin mischievously. Eimear still doesn't comprehend my sense of humour. She goes white, then her cheeks flush red. To keep her in suspense, I walk off in the direction of my *Jet Bubble,* starting to run in order to avoid the torrential water falling from the sky. She soon follows, as predicted. She is only doing her job, after all. Leaping into the *Jet Bubble,* pulling the glass top shut as fast as is possible, we glance at each other with a rush of adrenaline lighting up our eyes. Eimear moves to the rectangular back seat, where the servants belong, while I start the engine up and set the navigation to take me to Electrolaia. Taking off, I steer carefully, hoping that the storm doesn't decide to become electrical while I am getting past the cloud layer. While I am doing that, I contact Nada and explain that Illumaen matters keep me from Serpentin, signing off quickly before she can think of a comeback.

Finally, up in space, I look back at Eimear, who is looking up at the stars. Her hair has grown in the time I have known her, amazingly quickly. It falls to the middle of her back, the wild frizz now in soft curls. That could partly be because of me insisting that she keep her appearance dignified and elegant. Her eyes are a rich amber, and her skin is pale like bleached paper, pigmented by grey freckles.

"Do you know that you are beautiful Eimear?"

"What?"

"You're beautiful."

"Oh, well if you say so…"

"No, do not just believe something just because I say so. You have to look in the mirror and think: "I am pretty.""

"I don't. Usually I look in the mirror, and think: "Will I still be alive at the end of today?""

"That's terrible."

"Why would you care how I look? Or do you only eat beautiful people?"

"That's ridiculous. I don't see you and think about my next meal. I see a valuable assistant to me."

"If you say so…"

It is evident that it is extremely difficult to change the mentality of a person. I just hope that the Electrolans have minds that are open even a fraction.

Landing in the travel centre for the capital of Electrolaia, we step out into a remarkable world. I stand on the landing pad, drinking in the gorgeous sight. The buildings are gleaming in the light, lined with slick solar panels to harness the energy of the star they orbit. Vehicles powered by the roads they run on hum past, their drivers somehow connected to them, powering them too, egging them on to accelerate. It is almost mesmerising.

"You wonder how it all works?" a voice makes me jump.

"Yes…" I turn around, to see an incredible young woman. Her hair is this amazing powder-white, with a sheen that is iridescent. As she walks towards me, some of the strands shimmer the colours of the rainbow as they swing with her movements. That too is mesmerising. Wearing a baby blue bodysuit, the same shade as her eyes, with a shiny outer layer, and white knee length boots with a small heel, her entire aura is electric.

"You are Illumaen, the Ambassador?"

"Yes... I am Jade Firedancer." Reacting, she offers a hand for me to shake, her peach coloured skin running with sparks. Nervous, I tentatively return the offer. Our hands unite, and after an initial jolt, I feel something I have never felt before. The sharing of electricity.

"My name is Diamond," she smiles. "I am the Ambassador for Electrolaia. We have much to talk about."

"Indeed..." I beckon Eimear to follow as she leads me, still holding my hand, towards one of the strange vehicles, like a car in form. I sit in the passenger seat, Eimear is as usual relegated to the back, and Diamond takes the wheel.

"I will now explain how this all works," she smiles again at me. It is safe to smile here, good. It becomes wearisome after a while, for a natural smiler like me to suppress one.

"The road is powered by our central network, and it changes resistance and friction according to what the traffic flow is like. Kind of like traffic lights on Earth, where you grew up, only built into the road."

"Artificial intelligence?"

"In a way. We have a panel of fifty Electrolans who control the road. We transfer our commands electrically, and the road obeys. The same with the car. You see the steering wheel? It has a metal panel around the circumference. I put both hands on it, and it is ready to receive my instructions. If I think "go," it sets off." On cue, the car starts and moves off, indicating to pull out into the traffic.

"However, if I decide to drive into the car in front, then the road surface senses that there are two cars too close together, and it slows my car down, like now," she explains as the road roughens just enough to prevent a collision.

"How do you regulate the speed? Are there speed limits?"

"There are none. It is all relative to the speed of other vehicles. We can tell the car to speed up or slow down, and the road does the rest of the regulation."

"Intriguing..."

"It must be to an outsider. Many things here must be alien to you."

"It is remarkable..."

Parking at a diagnostic station which identifies and alerts the owner to any problems, we alight from the vehicle outside one of those solar skyscrapers, gleaming black, like all of the cars humming past on the road. On closer inspection, this structure is different: the edges of its hexagonal shape have a strip of light running their length, and the light zips up and down, changing colour as it goes, creating a dazzling show.

"This is where you and your aide will be staying, on the 7th floor. The chamber where our negotiations are to be held is on the 20th and top floor," Diamond walks us in through the door, with a geometrically decorated arch top, making the door into a hexagon of sorts. Eimear casts her eyes about somewhat nervously, hurrying along in my shadow. Electrolans greet Diamond as she walks past, confident in her manner and exuding an air of self-assuredness. Showing us into a lift, she presses the button for the 7th floor. I take hold of what I think is the handrail at hip-height which runs around the lift edges, excluding of course the side with the door. Diamond also grasps the rail. I get a jolt of electricity, and the lift moves up.

"Sorry, I should have warned you about that. The lifts are also powered by us."

"How do you possibly gain enough energy to do all of this?"

"There are two things you should know about our people: one, that we eat a whole lot more than say, an Illumaen. Two, we shut down for half of our day, which is 18 hours long."

"Your planet spins faster than Earth and Serpentin!"

"It does. It creates troublesome friction in the air and high winds regularly, but we harvest the electricity from our thunderstorms. That spare energy is mostly what we give the Illumaen Union at the moment in exchange for food and other materials."

"So, you are telling me that you give us your spare energy, and we give you our resources? And you are the one complaining. Many of our resources aren't simply by-products, we must work to obtain them."

"Steady, steady. We can discuss this tomorrow. For now, I will show you your room, and then we shall eat."

"Where?"

"On the second floor. Everyone in the building eats there. I will be at a table with another Electrolan you may want to meet."

"Thank you, I will meet you there in 10 minutes."

Wandering into the restfully decorated room, I suddenly feel very sleepy. The walls are a dark taupe, and the blackout curtains are, well, black. All the trimmings, including the skirting boards, are a metallic gold colour. My favourite part of the room, though, is the huge ceiling to floor window with a view of the electrifying city, the lights beaming, brighter it seems, with every passing moment. Eimear puts mine and her things on our respective beds, adorned with taupe and white bedcovers, and a gold runner.

"It must be the memorial for Chromium, it has worn me out."

"Well, we have to go and eat with the Electrolans before we go to bed," Eimear states, with only a trace of empathy, although she is also tired.

"True. I suppose that we must go."

I unpack my silky pyjamas, the sky blue Serpentin ones with silvery leaf motifs on them, before I stand ready at the door. Eimear follows suit, before we step into the hallway, trying to remember which way we came. Deciding upon the right, I look around me as I walk down the hallway, painted an intense black, but with silver diamond shapes, all linked, contrasting against the darkness, and a thin tube of light running horizontally along the middle of each wall, glowing light blue. Getting to the lift at the end of the corridor, I stop before we step in.

"How will we power it? Neither of us are Electrolan."

"You are telepathic. Can't you use that power?" Eimear comes up with a reasonable, but unattainable, solution.

"I guess it is a similar principle, but I don't know how..."

"Oh."

We stand awkwardly at the lift for a while, until an Electrolan comes along.

"Um, hi. We are from the Illumaen delegation. We were wondering if we are able to operate the lift?"

"You can hitch a ride on my electricity," he smiles, looking us up and down. We stand out like a sore thumb. Neither of us have bright hair, not even Eimear's vibrant red comes close. The young man we are in the lift with has dark green hair which fades to metallic silver at the ends.

"Thank you so much," I say, avoiding touching the metal bar while he focuses on moving the lift. It starts to drop suddenly, and we are all almost thrown off balance.

"Sorry, I am only 15 revolutions old, I am still working on control."

"That's okay. Is there any other way to get up and down?"

"Yes, there are stairs, beside the lift. The door sort of blends into the wall, it's hard to spot. I'll show you it when we get out."

"Thanks, otherwise we wouldn't be able to get from floor to floor without assistance."

"I think that's the idea. Electrolans like to keep track of their foreign visitors."

"Oh, okay." Perhaps I was overly optimistic about the concept of the Electrolans having open minds. Their borders seem pretty solidly closed to outsiders. They remind me a bit of humans: territorial, defensive, suspicious. They are going to be difficult to reason with.

He walks off to go about his business when we exit the lift on the second floor, but not before discreetly pointing to where the stairs are. I smile at him in gratitude, before walking through the plethora of tables, scanning for Diamond. Suddenly, a girl, probably 10 or 11, runs up to us.

"Hey, I'm Electra, you must be Jade and… Diamond didn't tell me your name."

I nudge Eimear to speak, so she obliges:

"I'm Eimear. Nice to meet you Electra."

"Diamond is over here…" she grins, taking my hand, almost electrocuting me in the process, and leading me to the side where the ceiling to floor window is. These windows are definitely my favourite feature in this building, covering the whole side of a room. I don't know how they make glass that strong. It is made of separate panes, with only one necessary in my room, but about 15 in this room, as it takes up the whole floor.

"Hello Jade, Eimear. Welcome to my table," Diamond gestures for us to sit down. Electra wants to sit beside Eimear, so I sit next to Diamond, instinctively edging away. I am genuinely afraid of her electrical power. It emanates constantly, and for some reason gravitates towards me, shooting out invisible charged particles that spark when they hit me. Eimear is equally apprehensive of the enthusiastic Electra, whose shiny navy hair and like coloured eyes with silver star-like flecks in the iris give her an intense look.

"I'll order for you, Jade. You must try the whole experience, and the expense is naturally in the category of Diplomacy Expenses. Have no fear, I am an expert in the food served here after 5 years."

"Okay, I guess I'll have to trust your judgement. Eimear doesn't eat much though…"

"Don't worry about your friend, I'll feed her up. She is a bit on the skinny side." Eimear visibly freaks out when she says that, instinctively looking straight at my stomach.

"It's okay Eimear, she doesn't mean it like that," I look at her sternly to stop her from telling Diamond that I am half-Serpentin. If Electrolans are similar to humans, they are likely to be prejudiced against me as a Serpentin.

"Haha, I was joking," Eimear forces a smile.

"You had us thinking you were genuinely scared there," Electra giggles.

The waiter comes over to take the order, and Diamond lists out so many dishes that I almost pass out with the concept of us eating all that. Not that I wouldn't manage, of course. I am, after all, capable of fitting a whole person in my stomach.

"Don't worry, everything is spread out over a couple of hours. We like to relax and enjoy each flavour."

"Oh, good."

Wow, most of their day is taken up with sleeping and eating, it is a wonder that they get anything done.

Eimear is still unsure about sitting beside Electra, who is showing her how she can light a lightbulb by touching each side. In fact, it fuses almost immediately, demonstrating her power.

"We haven't told you about Electra and her special role in our society yet," Diamond realises, and Electra looks up from her lightbulb breaking experiment.

"Really?" I smile. "Is she exceptionally talented in a certain area?"

"You can see that for yourself," Diamond takes the melted lightbulb from Electra, showing it to me. "Once or twice in a generation, a child is born with prodigious abilities in terms of electrical power. Electra has been training since she turned 10, when her power became clearly manifest.

"Training for what?" Now Eimear is intrigued.

"She will take over from the Electron Flow Regulator, currently a man who will retire in maybe 15 years. He operates the whole electricity supply of the planet and manages resources to export. Basically, in 15 years she'll be the brains of the outfit. It is a very demanding job, because she has to balance the electricity flow of the cities and towns, making sure there are no overloads. It is difficult to repair faults without the EFR to find them."

"I will be the next Electron Flow Regulator," Electra exclaims excitedly, almost getting tongue-tied in the process, turning to Eimear and taking her hands, zapping her with electricity - again.

"Ouch... Please. Let. Go." Eimear struggles to get the words out.

"Oops, sorry, I forgot you weren't Electrolan."

"That's okay," she regains her composure quickly.

The starter arrives, some sort of salad, that I deem safe to eat, so I dig in. I recognise many of the vegetables from having them on Illuma. From another planet in the Union I believe, that is agriculturally miraculous. I haven't been there yet though.

"Wow, that was a meal and a half!" I smile at Diamond, who is finishing a sweet, milky dessert like rice pudding. The past two hours have been quite the feast.

"You can sample some other dishes tomorrow, we eat like this basically every night," she smiles sweetly back. Electra gets up suddenly, asking: "Can I leave the table now?"

"Yes, of course. You need to sleep, tomorrow you are going to visit the main control centre. We can't have you making a mistake in your training and overloading all the junctions, can we?"

"No. See you tomorrow Jade, Eimear. I can show you some more of my tricks if you want."

Eimear opens her mouth, presumably to say that tonight was quite enough to see all her tricks, but I hurriedly step in to save us from embarrassment:

"Of course, we'd love to see that!"

Diamond rises too, and we stand as well. She puts out a hand for me to shake, and I am less tentative this time. I grasp her hand, and a current shoots up my arm. I look up to find Diamond soul staring at me. I consent for about a minute, before I break the stare and pull my hand away.

"Goodnight then. See you tomorrow on the 20th floor."

"Goodnight Diamond. It was a pleasure dining with you."

"I share your sentiments."

Eimear and I walk back to the lift, pushing gently on the wall beside it to reveal the entrance to the stairs.

Getting back to our room, I collapse on the bed, exhausted and uncomfortably full.

"I don't think I could cope with eating that much every night."

"How do you think I feel? I'm not even Serpentin."

"True. Anyway, it's best for us to get some sleep now," I change quickly with my back to Eimear while she does the same.

"Good idea," Eimear yawns and curls up in her bed like a cat, almost instantly falling asleep. I follow suit, closing my eyes and drifting off to sleep.

Electrolaia, and the Arrival of the Irritation

I awaken, feeling a little strange. Rolling out of bed, almost hitting my head on the bedside table, I right myself and stand up. Not even bothering to check the time, such is the reliability of my body clock, I stumble sleepily towards the shower. Stopping at the wardrobe on the way, I take my black blazer and trousers out, selecting an ivory-coloured shirt with black buttons to complete my classic Illumaen look. Hanging my outfit on the back of the door, I switch the shower on and leave my pyjamas neatly folded on the floor in front of the door. Gathering my thoughts for the day while I massage shampoo into my hair, I plan my line of reasoning to repair the alliance between Illuma and Electrolaia. Suddenly, I feel strange again, and an unwanted thought enters my head. 'Go away,' I will it to leave promptly. But it hangs around, still bothering me when I turn the water off and grab my towel. Twirling my heavy wet hair into a bun so it doesn't bother me, I slip my underwear on, frowning to rid myself of the intrusive thought which persists.

Buttoning my blouse, I pause halfway before continuing. Perhaps the thought has finally dissipated. Letting my hair down and squeezing the excess water from it with the towel, I comb it with my fingers before putting my blazer on and walking out of the bathroom. Eimear has only just woken up, knowing to set her alarm watch from Illuma to the time I exit the shower. She wanders in as I saunter out. Sitting on the bed, I put a pair of stud earrings on, with a polished green Jade stone in each. Fortunately for me, both Illumaens and Serpentins have a partiality for gemstones. I wear the Jade necklace from Chromium, undoing the first two buttons of my shirt to show it off. Stroking the pendant, I allow myself to become lost in thought, missing him. However, I quickly retrieve my focus, continuing about my preparations. There is no time in the life of a diplomat for missing friends.

I am just retrieving my black 2-inch heels from the bottom of the wardrobe when Eimear emerges from the bathroom. Sitting up from adjusting my shoes, the feeling I woke up with returns, all too distressingly. It's like there is a hollow in the pit of my stomach, a striking emptiness... The strange sensation of deep-seated hunger unnerves me. I look over at Eimear, who is retrieving something from her bedside table. Most likely her watch.

"Eimear?"

"Yes?"

"I need you to get out right now."

"Why? You look so pale, are you ill?"

"I just need you to leave the room before you get hurt, please!" The pitch of my voice shoots up, as Eimear finally gets the message and skedaddles, closing the door softly behind her.

I lie back, my hand on my torso. I have pretty much no idea what is happening to me. I have this intense and incapacitating urge to eat someone. Eimear is so slim; she would fit so perfectly in my stomach. I try desperately to shake the thought from my head. I am struggling even more than ever to adhere to the Illumaen way of thinking. I spend so much time on Serpentin that their ideals are beginning to influence me. Standing up cautiously, lightheadedly, I grab my files off the desk against the wall opposite the beds, glancing in the mirror to make sure I didn't forget to do something. Taking my light pink lip stick out of my makeup bag, I give my lips a coating of shimmering pink before opening the door.

Eimear is waiting for me just outside, leaning against the wall to the right of the door frame.

"Are you feeling okay now?"

"I think so. I think I just had another "Serpentin Moment," like the one I had a couple of weeks ago..."

"Was that when you were totally ready to eat me but then you stopped halfway across the room and turned away from me?"

"Umm, yes. This time it was stronger. So, the moral of the story is that next time I tell you to get out of the room, you should, or you'll end up my next meal."

"Of course, whatever my Hydra wants," Eimear snaps into her obedient servant mode. It annoys me when she does that, but it's her job.

"Thank you. Now, let's go and get some breakfast before I have to act all calm and measured in front of a panel of annoyed Electrolans."

"Great idea."

We make our way to the end of the corridor, remembering about the secret stairway, so Eimear pushes on the wall in several places before the concealed door swings open.

Wandering into the room we had dinner in last night, a glorious feast is laid before us. This is a breakfast buffet like no other. Food of every imaginable kind from the four corners of the Union decorates the long tables with rounded ends. I go for the fruit, primarily because I prefer to eat fruit for breakfast anyway, partly so that I don't accidently induce another "Serpentin Moment" by going near the meats. Perhaps that's why I was raised vegetarian... My aunt knew what would happen if I got a taste for animals, and by extension, humans.

Sitting at a table close to the window, I tuck into the kaleidoscope of colours on my plate while Eimear does the rounds of the tables, not actually putting much on her plate. Small girl, small appetite. As she walks back towards me, she is practically taken down by Electra, who catches her by the arm and jolts her with electricity.

"Ouch!" she yelps.

"Sorry, it's just that I'm so excited to see you again!" Electra buzzes with energy.

I diagnose her with hyperactivity. I decide to ignore her and finish my breakfast. Eimear is trying but failing miserably. Eventually, Electra waves goodbye, with a hand moving so fast it blurs, and leaves us in peace.

"She'd definitely be dead by now if she lived on Serpentin," Eimear comments, almost sounding like that would be a great thing.

"Watch that tone, you're supposed to be my PA, similar in disposition."

"But they don't know the other side of you Hydra…"

"I know Eimear. No need to highlight my shortcomings. I am acutely aware of them without any further emphasis."

"Sorry Hydra. Won't happen again Hydra."

"Jade…" I must be in a bad mood today. I try my best not to snap or use a cold tone with people. I think that my Serpentin side is dominating me today, which is not a good omen for the diplomatic negotiations ahead.

Making my way up to the top floor, Eimear leaves me to go to the room and do… something. I did give her some textbooks on alien languages, including Illumaen, because she has an interest in that sort of thing. Everybody has some area of excellence, even the slaves on Serpentin. Everyone has some form of aspiration or dream to start, even if it is later crushed by the turn of the wheel of fortune. Diamond joins me as I reach the top of the stairs, a little breathless from climbing 36 flights. She stands appraising me with a hand on her hip, dressed in a beautiful navy tailored jacket, navy wide leg trousers, and a silvery white V-neck top. That woman loves to show off her assets. Standing in the corridor, about to enter the conference room, we briefly make conversation.

"Morning Jade!"

"Morning Diamond, how are you faring this morning?"

"I was up all night preparing to rip your arguments to shreds," she grins somewhat manically, twirling a section of her hair around her finger as she speaks.

"I wasn't. I slept soundly."

"Overconfident and snobbish, like most Illumaens. I did actually think you were different. I sensed something else in you when I shook your hand. Something rather un-Illumaen…"

"Really? What do you mean?" This is me, a terrible liar, lying through my teeth to convince Diamond that I am entirely Illumaen.

"I heard a rumour of a half-Serpentin in a high office on Illuma. I thought we might get them. I guess we got you instead. Just as well for the welfare of your negotiations, because if you sent a half-Serpentin, we could easily rile them."

"You obviously have little faith in the concept of control."

"No, Electrolans live and die by control. However, other races, like Serpentins, are not so good at control. Even Illumaens do not measure up, in my opinion. After all, you don't have to control the electricity coursing through your body like us."

"Perhaps we control other things better than you."

"Ha! That just sums up what Illumaens think like. "Oh, we're certainly superior to all others. We have the 'right' to rule supreme, blah blah blah...""

She is trying to unsettle me before we begin negotiations. Quietly self-assured, I refuse to be moved, deciding instead to look extremely interested in my files.

"Oh, I see how it is. You're ignoring me. Am I white noise now?"

"I cannot listen to someone who tears apart rather than putting together."

"Fine. Rant over. Let's do this."

One by one, the five-person Electrolan delegation files in, sitting in a neat row at the spotless glass table gleaming in the starlight streaming through the window, which is of course floor to ceiling and making the fourth wall in the room, as in all of the rooms in the building. I am mildly intimidated, if not then vastly outnumbered. Yet another backhanded move by the Electrolans. They never told us that there would be five. I think for a fleeting instant to call Eimear for backup, but I dismiss that idea swiftly. It would make me look as if I had been cowed by the number who are against me. Sitting opposite the formidable line up, facing Diamond, who is in the centre, we commence our discussion...

"Look! These charts clearly demonstrate that the Union provides you with everything you need to thrive as a planet. Food, building materials, military protection, you name it, the Union provides it."

"Except for electricity," Diamond intensely maintains eye contact, trying to stare me into silence. I am, however, used to Nada glaring at me in expression of every emotion she feels towards me, so I am bothered little by Diamond's eyes.

"You will have to negotiate separately with all of the planets you require resources from. In addition, seeing as the Scytharians are currently planning their next offensive against this sector, and you are on the border with their territory, you will have no protection from the war that's about to start."

"We are capable of defending ourselves, and we are not so far beneath you that we cannot negotiate our own trade agreements. Maybe we are tired of being ordered around and having the things we need doled out to us as if we are weak and unable to handle our own affairs!"

"Illuma set up the Union to prevent rivalry and power grabs in this sector. We are protecting you from occupation, war, famine and poverty."

"That might be how you see it, but we see you as tyrannical leaders who oppress us and prevent us from holding any meaningful power, while crippling our ability to control our own resources. We want out, and that's the end of it!" The man sitting to the right of Diamond yells back.

I choose that particular moment to stay silent. The five people who were deafening me follow suit, somewhat confused.

"Perhaps now is a good time to take a break…" I state calmly, smiling ever so slightly at the puzzled, speechless delegation.

"Let's take a break guys! Re-group in 30 minutes!" Diamond takes charge, dismissing the delegation.

"Good job, but you still haven't convinced me," I smile mischievously at her.

"You will see it my way eventually..." she looks me in the eye, almost adding layers to the sentence she just uttered.

"You must enlighten me."

"Are you sure? I am a complex woman."

"I can see that. Maybe I can read your mind sometime."

"This evening."

"What?"

"This evening, you teach me how to read minds."

"What do I get in return?"

"I'll teach you how we harness the power of electricity. You are a good candidate, being telepathic."

"Oh okay."

"My quarters?"

"Fine... Where are they?"

"In the building opposite this one... I'll take you there."

"So, after dinner?"

"Absolutely."

'What just happened there? The vibes I get off Diamond are so confusing,' I think to myself as I make my way to get lunch, calling Eimear to meet me there. My stomach is indeed telling me it is time to eat. Still afraid of another "Serpentin Moment," I stride quickly to the restaurant/canteen (I am not sure how best to describe it).

"Hey Eimear," I swell with pride at her impeccable punctuality.

"Hello Hy... Jade. Sorry."

"It's fine. No one's actually listening. Did you do anything interesting this morning?"

"Not particularly... But I did read that book you gave me. Fascinating."

"I am glad to hear that you are investing in your intelligence."

"Sometimes I wonder if there's a point. After all, eventually I'll just end up in your stomach."

"Of course there is a point! You will acquire knowledge. We all die eventually. That doesn't mean that we should stop learning."

"I suppose…" slightly encouraged, she steps a little more cheerfully towards an empty table with me.

We take turns to go to the buffet, taking however much we fancy before returning, balancing our plates on the palms of our hands. Eimear once again barely eats anything. Xenonians evidently do not require very much sustenance. I, on the other hand, have a plate loaded to capacity with all sorts of food. Tucking in, I focus entirely on my plate.

"Are you okay Jade? You never take that much interest in your food."

"I am not really okay. My Serpentin half is exerting its power again."

"Oh, right. Should I stop talking?"

"It's fine."

In truth, it is not fine. I try to shake the desire out of my head, to no avail. Hauling my thoughts back to my Illumaen half, I struggle laboriously to get my mind-set over the border wall in my mind. I kind of get stuck, half on each side. I hate it when my head does that. This problem has gradually become more frequent as I am exposed to both cultures, and both try to claim me completely. Nevertheless, despite their seeming bigotry in relation to other races, the Illumaens are more tolerant of my Serpentin half than the Serpentins are of my Illumaen half.

Finishing in about ten minutes flat, I glance up at Eimear, who is about halfway through her meal.

"Is it safe now?" she asks.

"Umm… I think so… I hope so…" I rest my right hand on my upper abdomen, more contented than before. My thoughts are still impaled on the border between Serpentin and Illumaen.

"Any plans for this afternoon?"

"Electra is going to show me around."

"Have fun!" I giggle as Eimear rolls her eyes and sighs.

"I am going to take a walk around before I have to sit in that room again," I take my leave as she finishes her lunch and stands up, wary of Electra coming out of nowhere and pouncing.

I go downstairs to the reception area, with two large conference rooms on either side of the central foyer and a large desk where guests can check in to the hotel. It appears that it is the destination for high-flyers, as I see several Electrolans with the air of a CEO about them (I don't know if Electrolans call them something different). Among the throngs of people, pooled in small groups and scattered across the foyer, I spy a characteristically short Scytharian diplomat checking in. Moving in for a closer look, my curiosity sparked, I see him flirting with one of the Electrolan diplomat's PAs. Clearly, they have met before. 'So, what are you hiding Diamond? One of your fellows is negotiating with the Scytharians.'

I shiver as I think of what the Scytharians could do with the Electrolans' power. They could destroy our infrastructure by causing a power failure, or a major electrical fire. Why, they could even design a weapon to mass-electrocute us... I consider telling my father, Lawrence, about it. Then, I come to my senses. My mind is running away with me. Most of my hypotheses will never come to fruition. I will bide my time, and wait, and see what transpires. About to head outside, I notice that there is a veritable deluge of rain falling from the sky. I don't particularly want to get drenched, so I head back to the stairs and trek up what seems like hundreds of flights to get back to the top floor. By now my brain has settled, and I am back to the state of Illumaen serenity I so treasure. 'It would be best not to bring the Scytharians up during the talks this afternoon. After all, they are technically at war with us. I will simply pretend that I never saw that man.'

I settle myself once more in the seat I was assigned this morning. I organise my papers and ponder over which fights I will pick this afternoon. It is positively exhausting trying to have an educated conversation with these people, and even more so when it devolves into a shouting match. Diamond comes strutting in. I'm still not sure about her. She behaves so strangely I am still trying to ascertain her intentions.

"Oh, hey Jade. You're early."

"I eat quickly."

"Why so short with me? What happened?"

"Sorry. I am never sure who to trust."

"Don't worry, I'll soon fix that," she smiles disarmingly at me. It doesn't work, but she thinks it did. She strolls past behind me, stroking my long, silky hair as she does so. I pull it out of her reach, and she gives me a mock sad face. These Electrolans are certainly extremely expressive, and okay with a lack of personal space. If a Serpentin did that to me, they would soon find a hand around their throat.

"I am Illumaen, by nature conservative. I am unused to this social paradigm of spontaneously violating personal space."

"Aw, have you gone all shy on me? It's okay beautiful, us Electrolans are a very liberal people."

I am liking it here less and less. It makes me indescribably uncomfortable. It is inappropriate to call someone "beautiful," then have to negotiate with them on the subject of diplomatic issues. We probably shouldn't even speak outside of this room, at least by Illumaen standards. However, we are not on Illuma. We are on Electrolaia. And I believe that pretty much anything could happen in this place, no matter how fanciful it may seem.

Mercifully, the other four diplomats, all sharply dressed in well-made royal blue suits, with their metallic hair groomed to perfection, walk in. The men appear to have metallic hints in their hair, while the women have shiny or glittering hair. Diamond's almost glitters when the sunlight hits it. Electra's is shiny and smooth. I wonder how Eimear is... Leaning forward and putting one hand on top of the other, Diamond commences the afternoon's diplomatic shouting match, bringing me back to the task in hand.

By the time we wrap up for the day, the star illuminating Electrolaia is dipping below the horizon. The transition is almost imperceptible, as one of those infamous electrical storms has been raging all afternoon. I am thoroughly wrecked, and my head is spinning. Opting out of a social dinner with Diamond, I retreat back to my room and order something light to consume. I stare at my plate for at least half an hour before taking a bite; too tired to feel hungry, too tired to do anything but stare blankly into space. Eimear creeps in soon after I finish eating, worn out from Electra's rambunctious company.

"Tired?"

"More than ever before. You?"

"Shattered. Diamond is coming to collect me soon. I don't want to go and teach her how to read minds."

"Is she not going to teach you something in exchange?"

"Yes, but I'm not sure if my head can take it." I flop backwards onto the bed, stroking my belly to relax. Eimear sits on the edge of hers, and we look at each other for a while, unable to speak. Our brains are fried from the demanding day.

Just as I close my eyes, glad to unwind, a knock grates on my ears.

"Can you get that please?" I groan lazily.

Eimear trudges to the door to open it, and goes whiter than usual when she sees the person on the other side of the door...

The Mess

It is Nada.

Her first move is to grab Eimear by the shoulder, and she squeaks with terror. I start when she appears around the corner, clutching my poor servant by the arm.

"Preparing for dinner, are we?" she smiles slyly.

"No, I have just eaten," I stand up. I was already sat up and perched on the edge of the bed as a result of Eimear's squeaking.

"Shame. I would pay to see you eat your servant."

"However, you ARE interrupting my diplomatic mission for Illuma," I change the subject.

"Oops! I'm sooo sorry!" she sings sarcastically.

"I have commitments. I fulfil my responsibilities on Serpentin, and in return I expect to be left to fill my Illumaen role. Get out!" I snap.

"Hey! Just because you are the Hydra, it doesn't mean that you can shout at me."

"I am your superior. Get back in your place."

"Anyway, I came to tell you about the new invasion plans." Look who's changing the subject now?

"The NEW invasion plans? I didn't even hear about the OLD plans." I, as usual, have been left out of the loop.

"Oh, yes. Sorry about that." She isn't. "You know those Allaaraens…"

"Of course."

"You signed a peace treaty with them and derailed our masterplan."

"Yes, I did. They in return provide us with a section of Palladium to mine."

"We want it all. Allaara itself also has many precious minerals. And their people make wonderful meals. I had one myself, before you came along and destroyed everything. So, we have conceived a brilliant new plan."

"Watch your tone Nada. You do not have my permission to break the treaty or displace all those people."

"Displace? Who said anything about displacement? I will only be putting them where they belong, in our labour camps, or our mouths. That is their place. They are pathetic compared to us. Lower than animals in my opinion. They are so insignificant that they don't even have any means of defending themselves."

"That could be a sign of strength. They aren't afraid of anyone."

"Yeah, because of that dumb treaty. It's time to teach them a lesson they'll never forget… until we wipe out their sorry nation, that is."

"I have friends there. I will not stand for this. My answer is no!"

Nada is poised to launch another line of attack when Diamond breezes in. How did she get the key card? Never mind, I now have an enormous mess to clean up.

"And who are YOU?" Nada questions sassily.

"Diamond, the Electrolan diplomat. Who on Electrolaia are you?"

"Who am I?!" Oh no, she is going to yell. "I am Nada, the *Tradition Keeper* of Serpentin. I am briefing the Hydra on our latest military developments. What are you doing here?!"

"The Hydra? Don't be ridiculous." Diamond dismisses my title without a second thought.

"So, she didn't tell you about her status. I mean, you even put her in the same room as her servant… Absolutely disgraceful."

"She didn't. She came as a diplomat from Illuma. So Jade, you are the half-Serpentin!"

"I concealed that fact to avoid your nation's derision. I get enough abuse as an Illumaen."

"Hydra, if people mock you, you can reprimand them. I did that yesterday. My seamstress told me that she needed to add two inches to the waist of my jeans. What an insult! I let her make the adjustments… And then… I punished her," Nada displays her dislike of foreign languages as she switches from Illumaen to Serpentin, cutting Diamond out of the conversation.

Diamond looks at me for a translation of what Nada just said, and I instinctively look at Nada's abdomen. She is wearing a stretchy iron grey top tucked into her abyss blue jeans, so it is not hard to make out a bump in her outline. It's fairly obvious once you know what to look for. Her jeans still look a little small for her. I guess having a hobby like Nada's would affect the waistline eventually. I dare not tell her that though.

"Nada, that is not how I do things. I am Illumaen. I have certain sensibilities."

"It's natural justice. Eat or be eaten. Those who eat are the ones who succeed."

"How is that natural justice? People should be given a chance."

"That's your human upbringing talking now! I'm not stupid, I examined the humans' absurd justice system. Far too lenient. Except for the occasional dictator, they were on the right track."

"You just completely missed my point... You are dismissed Nada; I have an appointment with Diamond."

"Very well. I shall go to my room."

How did she get a room here? More importantly, how many people did she threaten to get this far? I sigh melodramatically, watching Nada stroll out of the room and down the hall with a condescending air. She infuriates me.

"That was quite random," Diamond smiles carelessly, confused at hearing us having a conversation in Serpentin.

"Indeed."

"You just switched back to Illumaen mode. How do you do that?"

"I just do. Sometimes it is harder to do than other times." Diamond is starting to get on my nerves too. Slightly, not as much as I thought she would. That could just be the product of Nada having left though.

"Come on, let's go! We have lessons to attend!" she takes my hand, sending an electric current through me again as she leads me down the hall and into the lift.

"So, this is where I live, on the top floor," she guides me into another skyscraper near to the hotel I am lodging in, very similar in design, but clearly a residential building rather than a hotel. A massive block of flats.

"See, I have an excellent view of the conference room," she points out of her floor to ceiling window at the gleaming building just across the car park.

"Oh, yes, in fact you have." Having been completely converted back to Illumaen mode, my tone is flat and lifeless, betraying my intense lack of interest. "I am sorry, I do not feel like instructing anyone this evening. Can I teach you tomorrow instead?"

"Oh, why of course, I don't mind at all. I can teach you about electricity conduction instead."

"No, seriously, I don't feel like it. Goodnight..."

I head for the door, but Diamond whirls me around and firmly plonks me on the bed. I very much dislike her forcefulness. I must make allowances though; she is after all of an entirely foreign culture. A good impression must be made.

"Sit on the bed and prepare yourself for your lesson," Diamond snaps her dark purple curtains shut, looking at me with a cheeky smile.

I perch apprehensively at the foot of the double bed, legs crossed, unsure of what to expect. I have a mind to march out of here and have done with it. Never mind, I am too tired to contemplate resistance anyway. Diamond takes her jacket off, casting it onto the pillows and abandoning it. Landing heavily beside me, she lies on the bed for a moment. Confused, I turn to check that she is okay. She pokes me in the small of my back, and I yelp with surprise.

"Did you feel the spark there?" she asks, sitting up properly.

"Yes, you have a very strong electrical current," I rub my back in confusion. How is she still this lively?

"I am really only average. Electra could do three times better, possibly more when she's older."

"It is still a whole lot more powerful than mine!" I laugh.

"Well, why don't we fix that?" she takes my left hand, then my right, completing a circuit between us. Uncrossing my legs, I surmise that the "lesson" has commenced. All I can feel is the energy travelling up my arms and into my chest, making me shiver.

"Now, try to focus on the current."

"Okay..." I close my eyes, concentrating on the electricity. I feel that it is starting in my left hand. Then it switches to my right hand without warning.

"You switched the direction."

"Good. You can feel it properly now. Now, try and do something with it. Slow it down, switch direction. Anything."

"Right..." I must look quite odd, frowning and squeezing my eyes shut to find what I am supposed to do. Focusing on the telepathic ability I have, I try to tell Diamond to switch the direction herself. She doesn't hear me, or she is ignoring me. Trying again, I try the same tactic on the current. 'Slow down, slow down,' I repeat in my head. The current slows almost imperceptibly, but Diamond notices.

"You just did something didn't you?"

"Yes. Well, I tried."

"It's working. The current is slowing down."

"Owww...." I feel a pain in my chest, accompanied by something akin to pressure. I try to breathe deeply, but it doesn't work in the slightest.

"Wait, I'll let go. You seem to have run into a bit of a problem," Diamond pulls her hands away from mine, but I am gripping them so tightly she has to use considerable force.

"What happened there?!" she stands back, not sure how to respond.

"I... Don't know," I cough, still trying to breathe.

"That never happens with Electrolans."

"Have you considered that our physiology isn't at all compatible? I am Illumaen."

"And Serpentin."

"Do not bring that subject up, please," I sigh wearily.

A staged pause follows, as I regain my composure, and Diamond stares at me, dying to quiz me about being Serpentin.

"Oh alright, shoot. What do you want to know?" I capitulate.

"Who is that woman you were talking to?"

"That is Nada. She is basically my babysitter, to make sure I project the right image of the Serpentin Empire at all times. She detests my Illumaen side."

"She seems pretty ruthless. I don't know that much Serpentin, but I conclude that she was telling you about something diabolical she had done."

"Yes, well, she is unhinged. I wouldn't cross her; she might well try to eat you."

"Right... How does that work anyway? The eating people?"

"We swallow them whole, and usually have to rest while they digest. That can take 24 to 72 hours. Nada takes perverse pleasure in keeping her victims alive for as long as possible."

"O...Kay... Right. What does it feel like? To be eaten alive?"

"Don't ask me, I have no idea."

"Hmm... Did you never ask anyone?"

"I don't know anyone who lasted to tell the tale." I'm not about to just go and ask Alina about that traumatic event about a month ago.

"And how do they stay alive for that long? Would they not suffocate?"

"Haha, I asked Nada that. She simply said: "We swallow a lot of air while we devour our prey." Maybe we just keep doing that to give them air..."

"You don't know? You are some Serpentin."

"Excuse me, I've only ever eaten one person."

"You'll have to do better than that as an excuse," she leans in closer to me, whispering in my ear. I swat her and decide that now is the choice moment to get out.

"Maybe I can try and teach you telepathy tomorrow. I am too exhausted to do it currently."

"Oh, okay..." the disappointment saturates her vocalisation. "Well, I'll come and get you at the same time tomorrow. And... maybe you can wear something a Serpentin would? I'm curious to see how the culture works."

"Curiosity killed the cat," I state bluntly, before turning and walking quickly out of the room. I do not stop to draw breath until I am safely in my own lodgings with Eimear. I am unused to the close proximity Diamond insists upon. I guess sharing electricity requires closeness, so

Electrolans are accustomed to leaning close to others when communicating. Us Illumaens have no need for such intimacy. We respect the area around others so as not to crowd them.

"You look... startled," Eimear attempts conversation.

"No." I am uncharacteristically short with her, as I cut her off, and get ready for bed in my usual efficient manner. My Illumaen manner. Finally, I crawl into bed, sliding between the sheets and lying flat on my back, shattered.

"What happened to you Hydra? You are shaking."
I peer down at my hands in the semi-darkness, which are lying either side of me on top of the duvet. Eimear is right. I am shaking.

"Umm... Diamond tried to teach me how to control electricity. It didn't go well."

"Don't do that again."

"Thank you for your statement of the blatantly obvious," I smile just a little. Of course, I have forgotten the Serpentin interpretation of a smile. Eimear retreats under her duvet, lying very still.

"Sorry..." my voice dissipates as I turn over onto my right side, facing away from her. Closing my eyes, my mind is running in circles again. The Illumaen curse, I call it. Eventually, the runner becomes too exhausted to continue, and I fall asleep.

Diplomatic Navigations

I sleep too soundly, unaware of the passage of time and the necessity to rise. Eimear has to wake me up. She nudges me nervously, whispering:

"Hydra, Jade, you need to get up. Negotiations start in an hour."

"Hmm…" I groan, intending to ignore her. Standing over me, she wracks her brains for a solution to the problem. She has already opened the curtains, allowing the morning light to sting my eyes. I simply shut them again. She gives me a shove, almost causing me to roll off the bed.

"Get up!" she uses her normal volume.

I persist in my ignorance, covering my ears with my hands.

"Huh…" she sighs. "Time to try the last resort I guess," she makes sure I can hear her. She pulls the covers off of me, leaving them in a heap on the floor.

"Nooo…" I curl up, stubborn in my desire to sleep.

"Right, okay, the final, desperate effort," she sighs, at a loss as to how to handle this alien situation.

I do not see or hear her, but she takes her socks off, and rolls me onto my back. Waving her foot near my mouth, I still do not stir. She parts my lips with her toe, and sticks her foot in my mouth. I cough with surprise and try to open my eyes. I feel my jaw popping, and her ankle in the back of my throat. Rubbing my eyes, I sit up, accidentally making her whole lower leg slide into my oesophagus. Eimear starts to panic as I flip her onto her back, guiding her other leg into my moist gullet. She starts scrambling away from me, the rapid movement bringing me to my senses. She looks most unimpressed.

"Now I have to change my trousers!" she complains loudly to drown out the sound of me putting my jaw back in place. She hates that sound.

"And I have to wash my mouth out. Did you wash your feet?"

"Yes, I did shower this morning. You slept through that. You have 45 minutes to get ready for your conference this morning."

"Yikes! Why didn't I wake up?"

"You must have been completely wiped out after yesterday. You never need waking up."

"The foot in mouth tactic worked superbly."

"You almost decided to have me for breakfast."

"That's what you're there for isn't it?" I grin mischievously.

Stumbling over to the wardrobe, I select a black knee-length body hugging dress with a high neckline and a scoop back. Wearing my black jacket over it, I complete the look with a thick black belt, which has a gold circular buckle. Washing my face quickly, I pat it dry and then run to grab some gold drop earrings in the shape of a double helix. Pulling my black patent Mary-Jane heels on, I glance in the mirror. I look uncharacteristically pale, more Serpentin than Illumaen. Dabbing concealer around my eyes, liquid foundation on the rest of my face, and a little gold-hued eyeshadow on my eyelids, I finish the look with a pale pink lipstick and a touch of blusher. Now I look alive. Eimear throws my folder of papers at me, presumably to test my reflexes. I catch it with ease.

"See you at lunch time, be good, don't let Nada eat you, etcetera, etcetera..." I wave Eimear goodbye as I hurry to the stairs and trot up them. It is difficult to run at any speed wearing heels.

"Hello Jade, you seem flustered. Are you worried that we would beat you to a pulp at the negotiation table?" Diamond sniggers playfully.

"I slept late."

"Was yesterday all too much for you?" she patronises.

"I believe the electrocution in the evening was a contributing factor." I opt for the flat and dispassionate tone. Diamond loses interest, as I turn my nose up at the bait she has dangled before me. The four men comprising Diamond's diplomatic entourage arrive, and so we sit down, glaring at each other in suspended quiet before commencing our morning of debates.

At the lunchtime recess, I am yanked back into my Serpentin life by Nada, who is practically standing on the threshold between the room and the hall, waiting for me to finish. If she was a kid, she would have her nose pressed up against the glass door.

"Finished playacting with your friends? Time for real Empire Management."

"Nada, my job on Illuma is equally important to me as my role on Serpentin." I dare not tell her that I deem it more important. She would go ballistic.

"Well, it's not a real job," she digs.

"It's more real than the pathetic approach to "Empire Management" on Serpentin."

"Hey, I am the *Tradition Keeper* around here, I get to have an opinion on our management, not you."

"I am the head of management..."

"Don't you dare use that line!" Nada has a notoriously quick temper, as is evidenced by her actions. Sometimes I annoy her, just for the reaction. However, I have had an arduous morning, and my patience is slipping away from me. I turn on my heels and walk away, leaving Nada with her mouth half open in surprise. It is simply a marvel to witness Nada with her mouth open without someone nearby to put in it. Standing and watching me for a moment, she then trots quickly to my side. This is doubtless only after she clocks that I am going to eat lunch. Food is a particular weakness of hers, as you may have gathered.

We hitch a lift with Diamond, who glares distrustfully at Nada. Nada narrows her eyes back, equally distrusting. I stand awkwardly in the middle, unsure if I should break up a fight, in the event of one starting. As the lift glides to a halt, so well-honed are Diamond's skills, it is evident that Nada is deeply disturbed by the concept of somebody who can stare back. Attempting to claw back the upper hand, she bares her teeth in a flash of a snarl, stopping short of growling. Diamond doesn't break eye contact until she steps elegantly out of the lift, striding away as confidently as ever.

"I hate her," Nada breathes menacingly in Serpentin.

She is powerless. Diamond and I can converse because all in the Illumaen Union must learn Illumaen in school. Electra speaks excellent Illumaen too, and I taught Eimear. I feel more comfortable speaking Illumaen. It is similar to Latin, and easy on the ears. Electrolan is faster, but still a soft language. Serpentin, however, is a harsh, clipped language. I would even say it makes it sound as if we are constantly arguing. It is basically the only language Nada speaks. She learnt the minimal amount of my Earth language, and Illumaen, to get me started, but now that I have learned Serpentin she refuses to speak any other language. She cannot breathe threat and murder at Diamond, because she wouldn't understand. So, she can only use body language to intimidate her. Which doesn't make the slightest difference.

"Hello Eimear, on time as usual. Excellent," I greet her in Illumaen.
"Speak to your slave in Serpentin!" Nada is further infuriated.
"Fine. Eimear, did you get us a table?" I bark in Serpentin, apologising with my eyes. She scurries off to a window seat, and pulls a chair out, gesturing for me to sit down.
"Just as I commanded you – Excellent. Nada will join us."
I sit where there is a view out of the window onto the streets. Nada stations herself opposite me, staring at Eimear to serve us.
"I will go and obtain your meals. What would you like?"
"Just salad for me, and some of that cool fluffy bread over there..." I indicate to where the bread selection is.
"As much protein as is in this place. I didn't eat anything yesterday," Nada smiles at Eimear, sending her running.

"I can't believe you still have her. You must be malnourished," Nada appraises my lean figure.
"Well, she is an exemplary servant. She tried to feed herself to me this morning."

"Then why is she still out here? And not in there?" She points to my stomach.

"I decided it would distract me and the Electrolan delegation if I was trying to digest at the same time as negotiating. We are trying to sort out a veritable diplomatic catastrophe. You have no idea how vital it is that this nation stays in the Union."

"Just threaten them. That ought to stop them from staging a mutiny."

"You are so… Serpentin!" I raise my voice for the first time in quite a while.

"And you are so… Illumaen!" Nada yells back, standing up and slamming her palms on the glass table.

"Woah, guys, what's going on?" Electra comes to join us at the table, studying Nada suspiciously.

"And who are YOU?" Nada looks down at her. Electra comes to Nada's shoulder, and my chest. Both Serpentins and Illumaens are tall, but I am easily a head taller than Nada.

"Electra," she grins mischievously, offering a hand. Nada makes as if to shake it, or grab it, I am not certain which. And boy does she get a shock. I cover my face trying not to burst into fits of laughter as Nada jumps out of her skin, yelping in surprise and pain.

"What is this sorcery! I hate this place. And I hate you, half-Illumaen, for bringing me here!" she screams in her embarrassment.

"Hey, you address me as Hydra madam!" I snap into Empress mode, grabbing her arm and sitting her down with a snarl. Nada sits sullenly, her fingers laced, looking at her knees.

"I am so sorry about that Electra. She deserved that shock," I smirk.

"I saw that she needed bringing in line," she giggles sweetly, with a cheeky spirit in her eyes.

Electra makes as if to sit beside Nada, who growls at her.

"Come and sit beside me Electra, Eimear will sit beside Nada," I ameliorate the tense situation. Eimear is clearly displeased with where she has been located but bears it nobly. Nada picks grumpily at her food, in a sulk. I ignore her, and happily eat my salad. Electra has already eaten, and so produces a lollipop she smuggled from somewhere and sucks on it, waiting for us to finish with a bored expression. I clear my plate in ten minutes, as I do not have to speak in between mouthfuls. Eimear finishes just after me, seeing as she doesn't eat anything anyway. Electra, ecstatic that she can finally talk at us, starts to explain at one hundred miles an hour what she did that morning. Nada demonstrates terrible table manners by crunching into a bone. Well, terrible manners by Illumaen and Electrolan standards. I kick her under the table, fuelling her angst.

"Hey guys, how is everyone doing?" Diamond breezes to our table.
"Nada can't stand you. Steer clear please."
My diplomatic head is back on, now that I have eaten.
"Hey, Jade," she leans in close to me, bent over with elbows on the table, her eyes gazing into my soul. "We have five minutes to get back up to resume our negotiations."
"Diamond, can you please get out of my face? Illumaens value personal space."
"Oh, sure honey." She straightens up, flicking her hair and hitting Nada in the face with it. Anyone who has ever been hit in the face with hair knows how sharp the strands are. Nada shoots daggers at her, which she disregards.
"I will be with you presently," I warn her off. Mercifully, she turns and walks away, leaving us in peace.

"Eimear, can you make sure that Nada doesn't interfere with my meeting?"
"Sure…" she takes Nada by the arm, pulling her away and hopefully to her room. Nada limply complies, owing to the sleeping powder I sneaked into her drink while Electra was conveniently directing her attention elsewhere. Admittedly, I possibly misjudged the dose, so the effects were delayed. I had to estimate her weight, which may have increased since I formulated the plan a week ago. An Illumaen diplomat must always plan ahead.

"What's wrong with her?" Electra looks quizzically at me.

"For future reference, her name is Nada. I gave her a sedative so she would not hurt anyone."

"Who is Nada?"

"She is a Serpentin. She does not speak Illumaen or Electrolan, so she will not understand you if you say something to her."

"So, why is she here? With you…" Children are far too curious for their own good sometimes.

"I am half-Serpentin. Nada follows me around making sure I behave like a Serpentin. I am important on Serpentin, you see."

"Oh, okay… How do you behave like a Serpentin?"

"Basically, I have to be mean to people, and shout at them, and things like that."

"You don't act like that at all. You act like an Illumaen, all sensible and polite."

"I think it is better to act like an Illumaen."

"I think so too. I don't like how Nada acts."

"Well, Electra, that makes two of us. I am sorry, but I must return to my meeting."

"Can I visit you and Eimear after I finish my lessons for the day?"

"I might not be there, but you can come and hang out with Eimear. She probably gets lonely on her own all day."

"Great!" Electra pushes her chair under the table and skips off to her next lesson.

Sitting up in the chair that I have grown accustomed to over the past day and a half, I ready myself once more to chase my tail, as it were, trying to win the Electrolans over to the wider view the Union holds on the subject of their departure.

A Jewel of a Meal

Our day's discussions continue well into the evening. Diamond put a stop to them after one of her posse started staring mindlessly at a corner of the room. We are all spaced out from the mental exertion of presenting argument after argument, getting nowhere. However, I feel that I have made some form of a breakthrough. I showed them a digital simulation of what would happen if the Scytharians attacked them, and there was no Union on standby to assist them. I designed it to be raw, and as jarring as possible. They visibly flinched several times while it was running. So, perhaps tomorrow they will have had adequate time to mull over the consequences of their exit from the Union.

"I'll come and meet you outside your room in 30 minutes? I will go and get changed."
"Of course, see you there."
"Oh, and don't forget... Wear something more Serpentin."
"I have not forgotten."

I collapse on my bed, staring up at the high white ceiling. I allow my eyelids to close, just for a moment, as I contemplate my next move. My mind is racing from talking all afternoon. It feels like I was mostly only having a discussion with myself. These Electrolans are deaf to outside opinion. Nevertheless, they appeared receptive to visual aids. Perchance, I could use that to catch their attention.

Eimear carefully brings me back into the present, asking what I am to wear this evening.
"Diamond wants me to wear something Serpentin..."
"Oh, I know just the thing you require... I snuck a couple of outfits into your suitcase, knowing the flighty nature of your ambassadorial work."
It is so wonderful to have a servant who anticipates every possible need. She lays a pair of low-rise dark wash jeans on the bed, alongside a lacy white crop top with thick straps.

"I hope that top isn't too short," I sigh, knowing instantly that it is. I take my shoes and dress off, having to swap my bra for a dainty white one. Stretching the top on, it barely covers my bra, save a thin band of lace on the bottom. I pull the jeans over my legs, pleased that they at least fit snugly, a straight leg style as opposed to skinny. I cannot abide skinny jeans; they never seem to fit me correctly. Seeing as the only two shoe options are my heels and a pair of brown boots, I select the boots for comfort. Retrieving my brown leather jacket from its hanger, I leave my jewellery behind on the table in front of the mirror. Knowing Diamond, she might pull a stunt and damage it. Zipping the jacket over my midriff, I feel less exposed.

"How do I look?"

"Gorgeous, but even more amazing if you open that jacket."

"Eimear, I am not going on a date. I am going to teach someone how to mind read."

"She asked to see what Serpentins are like. This is how they dress - to show off. Diamond does the same. Women like to feel good about themselves."

"That much is true."

Suddenly, there is a short rapping at the door, and I quickly swipe a shimmering brown lipstick on before answering the knock. Diamond stands, one hand on her hip, poised to greet me. She is wearing a stunning hot pink skater dress with a high round neckline, a lace overlay and short lacy sleeves.

"Leather, huh? Is that very Serpentin?"

"Not the most Serpentin thing on me, but a feature of most of my casual outfits."

"Seriously? You are using that Illumaen tone with me again. Lighten up."

Funny, how I so want to be rid of my Serpentin side, and everyone around me accepts, or encourages it. That said, I still do not trust

Diamond. There is something unusual, terrifying, in her. A gravity which draws you in like a neutron star. Dazzling, but lethal.

The heavy scent of perfume hits me as soon as I enter her room. I am sure Diamond has to be wearing some, because no-one sprays this much perfume in a room without getting some on them. It is sultry, with floral notes and a rich woody base. The smell is almost intoxicating.

"What is that heavenly scent?"

"My perfume. You will be able to smell it on me when you are teaching me to use telepathy."

"Yes, sure."

I feel dizzy from the assault on my nose. I have exceptionally sensitive smell. Illumaens have masterfully honed senses. It enables them to fully appreciate the world around them, and notice things other species do not. I sense that something is not as it should be. I smell a rat, as the Earth saying goes. Diamond sits me down on the edge of her bed, facing the window. Smothering her lips in a fresh coat of pink gloss to match her dress, she joins me, soul staring again.

"So, to start, take my hands," I attempt to distract her, offering my hands, preparing myself for the electrical intrusion.

"Okay..."

"Try to relax, your mind is very active at the moment."

"How can I relax? I'm excited to learn." she giggles playfully.

"Stop being frivolous and focus Diamond."

"Alright, alright." I can feel her mind slowing down, ceasing to jump from thought to thought. I sigh with sheer relief. It is tiring to read a hyperactive mind.

"Right. Now you are ready. You can use your knowledge of electricity to help you. Try to pinpoint a feeling. It is more abstract than a thought and should be easier to identify."

I try to concentrate my energies into one emotion to make it easier. Diamond closes her eyes, frowning in concentration.

"You are calm?"

"Very good. That is the easiest emotion to read. Try another one."

"Oh… you are… tense. Stressed?"

"Excellent. You are catching on quickly." She is certainly picking it up more rapidly than I anticipated. Caught off guard, I let my control slip for just a moment.

"You are… hungry."

"How did you get that?"

"It felt like you had a mind slip."

"Indeed, my barrier slipped. Well detected."

"And why might that be?" She smiles sweetly, probing for further information.

"Well, I have not yet eaten this evening."

"Oh, poor you!" Here she goes again with the sarcastic tone. I hate sarcasm, it reminds me of Nada.

"Back to the task at hand Diamond, how about you give me access to an emotion you are feeling. Telepathy is reciprocal."
She reads as on edge, tensing up and buzzing with anxious anticipation.

"Take a chill pill Diamond, you are very tense."

"Huh, really? Why am I tense? Tell me…" she giggles playfully.

I read her train of thought, and instantly shut down. There is something off about her for definite.

"I think we need to take a break. Your brain will tire quickly learning this skill. I used to get tired from reading emotions before I understood my Illumaen heritage and how to operate my gift of telepathy."
I gently extricate my fingers from between hers, leaving her, eyes closed, deep in thought. I lie back on the bed, breathing deeply. I feel quite odd. Perhaps the perfume is too strong, and it is making me dizzy. Diamond turns to me to check that I am still awake. I am indeed awake, though stunned by what I read just before.

"Can somebody… volunteer?" a glint in her eye betrays her motives.

"Volunteer?"

"Well, has anyone asked to be eaten? I want to know what it feels like."

"It's a one-way ticket Diamond. Nobody wants to die slowly and painfully."

So, she was going to verbalise her bizarre idea eventually.

"Hmm... Well... I can be the exception to the rule..."

"No."

"You want it really. Come on, just eat me..." She leans in playfully, locking eyes with me. Out of the corner of my eye I notice her hand floating stealthily towards my torso.

"No. Stop, Diamond."

Unzipping my jacket, she places her hand flat on my abdomen. She slowly begins to move it in circles. She smiles upon feeling my stomach grumble. I roll away, curling up.

"Aw, come on. How often in your life will someone offer themselves to you, Hydra? Most exalted Empress, do give me this honour..."

Well, I mean, I am in need of food... Wait, what in the galaxy am I thinking? I violently shove the idea away.

"No, Diamond. I am on official business on behalf of Illuma - I am not about to risk the relationship between our planets to indulge your imbecilic whim."

"Aw, you've gone all Illumaen on me again..." Her voice is sickly sweet, her tone oozing like honey. "Oh sweetheart. Why do you protest so?"

She creeps her hand up to my lips, trying to open my mouth. I am dazed, and my head is starting to throb. There is something in the air, I am sure of it. Shaking myself out of my trance, I stand up abruptly.

"No! I am going to retire for the night, I feel unwell. Goodnight," I state curtly.

"Come on! Your voice says no, but you're dying to say yes..."

"My no means no. Goodnight Diamond.

I speed walk in the direction of the door, leaving Diamond gazing after me, stunned into silence. I have just pressed my earpiece to speak to Eimear when Diamond tackles me, slamming me face-first into the carpet.

"So, you want to play it this way huh? You have some nerve, *Hydra*." The mocking in her intonation when she says "Hydra," tips me over the edge. I flip her over, knee on her chest, pinning her down by the wrists. My hands hurt from her trying to push me off with her electricity.

"Don't you dare disrespect me like that again, do you hear? I am leaving NOW, and if you try to stop me, I will doubtless do something reprehensible."

Brushing myself down, I stand up, almost smacking straight into Eimear, who got to the door at just the opportune moment.

"Hey, Eimear, you got here just in time."

"Why? What happened to your face?? All I heard was an almighty crash."

"Diamond happened to my face. She slammed me into the carpet. She wanted me to eat her."

"Liar! I had to restrain your mistress, she almost ate me," she yells, threatened by the truth.

"Jade, really? You should have eaten before coming here," Eimear frowns, troubled.

"I did not try to eat her. I am, however, in no position to defend my case. I feel sick."

"You are sick alright! I am one of the highest officials on Electrolaia, and you decided I'd be better off as food!"

"No Diamond, you decided you'd be better off as a meal. It would have been a jewel of a meal no doubt... But your wish for martyrdom would have been completely lost. Your people would think you weak, for having been subdued. The Illumaens would tighten their grip on

Electrolaia, as their primary argument is that you cannot fend for yourselves. I… honestly wouldn't remember you for more than a week."

That was a lie. The guilt would plague me for months. Best to remain consistent in proving a point though.

"I got a strong smell of perfume when I came in here… Should I send it to Illuma for testing? It made me feel ill," Eimear wrenches the subject around like a driver swerving to avoid a tree. Anything to avoid the topic of the Serpentin psyche.

"Yes… The perfume… You are very perceptive Eimear. Yes, catch some in a jar and make sure it gets to Illuma. There has to be a drug of some description in it."

"Tailored no doubt to Illumaens."

"I am positive that they will unearth something. I never liked Diamond; I could never be sure of her intentions," I glare pointedly at Diamond as I speak, as if holding the edge of a sword to her throat.

"I'll inform you of my intentions then!" Diamond retorts, fed up of the conversation not revolving around her. "I wanted to discredit you, so that we wouldn't have to continue with these stupid talks. All we want is our liberty. We don't care what you can offer us, in return for our complete devotion. Nothing is worth as much as our freedom. I hoped to show that you Illumaens can be driven to emotional extremes. I wanted a man to come, so that I could make him lustful or jealous. Then you showed up. There was very little I could do, until I found out that you are half-Serpentin."

"Why did you try and kill yourself then?"

"I planned to get out once you passed out. There was a tranquiliser in the perfume."

"I know, I could smell it. Now I can also feel the effects taking hold. Thanks a lot!" I quip sarcastically.

"Well, by the morning all of Electrolaia will hear of my heroic escape from the belly of the beast, and you won't be able to get out of bed."

"I tried to help you! You do not listen to reason. You are so used to charming your way to the top that you refused to listen to my pitch."

"Ha! Your policies you tried to force on us? We've had enough of Illumaen facetiousness. We want to rule ourselves, that's that. Do you have any more suggestions now, *Hydra?*"

"No, I do not! You have annihilated any hope of diplomatic discussions between us at this stage. Good luck in dealing with the rest of the Illumaen Council. Goodnight!" I storm out, Eimear in tow.

Eimear and I retreat to our building. I collapse before I reach my bed, face-planting on the floor. Eimear drags me to my bed, before pulling me onto it. She is stronger than she looks.

"Right, I want the truth," she sits cross-legged on her bed, staring me dead in the eye.

"It was going okay. Diamond is pretty good at discerning emotion. Then she started to mess around, telling me that I was hungry, and that she could be of service in that matter."

"What did you do?"

"What do you think? I attempted to make myself scarce as quickly as possible. Then she tackled me, and decided to mock my title."

"Ah, right. Did you take the bait?"

"Sort of, almost, kind of..."

"What?!"

"No, not like that. I simply restrained her without injury, and you came in just as I stood up again."

"Do you think that she will actually tell everyone her version of reality?"

"I have no doubt whatsoever."

"What are we to do?"

"One thing is for certain, there is no need to call for one of Illuma's big cover ups."

"Huh?"

"Like the damage control for my disappearance. They engineered a whole alternate reality specifically for my poor Aunt Skifa. I still write her letters from "Japan" where I am studying "Business.""

"Okay, that was very random information… time for you to go to sleep I think."

"Don't worry about Diamond, I'll fix it tomorrow…"

My vision blurs, and my eyelids feel weighed down. It comes on so suddenly that I flop sideways. I feel Eimear's palms supporting my shoulder, pushing me gently back onto the bed. I roll myself into a self-soothing foetal position, one arm on my knee, the other beside my face. That's the last thing I remember.

I fall out of bed, striking my head on the bedside table and landing on my back.

"Owww…" I grumble, getting on my knees and pawing the mattress to pull myself to a standing position. My head is pounding, and I feel so ill I wonder if I am dying. I crawl to Eimear, shaking her awake.

"Huh…" she takes a moment to achieve full consciousness. "Oh, yes my Hydra, how may I be of service?" she sits up attentively, prepared to please her mistress.

"I feel like I am dying. My head is killing me."

"You look hungover."

"That really helps Eimear, thanks."

"I will send the perfume sample to Illuma today. We will know by the evening what its effects are."

"It's no good to me this evening!" I shriek, before whimpering in agony.

"Calm down Jade, let's get you to the shower. You'll feel better after that."

She speaks in a low, gentle voice, so as not to irritate my sensitive ears. Putting one of my arms across her shoulders, she helps me to the bathroom. By the time we get to the door, I have found my feet, although I am still unsteady. Eimear leaves me in the bathroom with my towels and the black and white suit I wore the first day I went to the negotiation table here.

Stepping cautiously into the shower, I close the glass door behind me. 'Now what do I do?' I endeavour to focus my mind. My surroundings are fuzzy and jigging around. Squinting, it takes me four attempts to press the button on the wall below the shower head. I adjust the temperature dial until icy water cascades onto my shoulders. I stay there until I shiver, drenching my whole person in the almost frozen liquid. Splashing my face, I switch the shower off again. Almost tripping over the lip of the shower tray, I take hold of the shower door to avoid falling on my face.

'Eimear was right, my head has improved slightly,' I sigh ponderously as I dry myself, pulling my underwear on. I am just doing the strap up on my bra when I all of a sudden feel nauseous again, so much so that I induce myself to vomit in the toilet. Throwing up, as I previously mentioned, does not come naturally to Serpentins. Besides, I haven't eaten anything yet, so there's nothing but bile. Eimear, alarmed at hearing me retching, knocks urgently at the door.

"Are you alright Jade?"

"What does it sound like?" I cough.

I have no time to talk. I pass out on the floor, feeling like death. If I ever get a chance, I will suffocate Diamond. Or perhaps almost suffocate her a few times, before finishing the job.

Eimear nudges me awake, unintentionally, as she dresses me, trying to get my trousers into the correct position. It is evidently difficult to dress someone who is out cold.

"Hmm…Huh?" I mumble unintelligibly at her.

"Just your top now, then you really need to get your act together," she grins at me, her eyes mirthful. She is holding back a laugh. No one has ever seen me in such a ridiculous state. I have never been in such a ridiculous state before, come to think of it. I submit to being served for once, going limp again, allowing her to make all of the effort, straightening my shirt out on my floppy form. She grunts as she drags me onto the carpeted floor of the main room, propping me up against a wall.

"Now, do you still feel ill?"

"A bit. I no longer want to regurgitate my digestive system, if that is what you mean."

"You could've just said "puke my guts out.""

"That is not very Illumaen."

"Yep, you are better. Get up, lazy!"

She grabs my shoulders, and I brace myself against her as I stagger to my feet, gripping her upper arms tightly.

"Okay, now let go, and get upstairs! Recall, you have damage control to do."

"I need to eat before going up. Otherwise, Diamond is in mortal danger."

"Let me find something…" Eimear scurries off, searching the room for concealed sustenance. Finding none, she stands in the middle of the room, looking a little confused and in a ponderous state of mind. I give up, grabbing my files and making for the door.

"No, wait!"

"Did you find something?"

"No, I am just a bit concerned."

"You know what? I'll be okay."

"Are you sure?"

"Fine, I will drink a bottle of water to fill my stomach. That should be enough, and if not, I can drink more."

"Here, I have a glass," Eimear shoves it under my nose. I down the whole glassful in one go. She hands me a bottle of water, and I drink it while hurrying down the corridor to the stairs, leaving little dents in the carpet with my heels.

An unsuspecting Electrolan happens upon me while I am psyching myself up to go up all those steps, so I ask if I can hitch a ride in the lift with them to the 20th floor.

"Are you part of the foreign delegation?" she pierces me with her dark brown eyes.

"Yes…" I stop, not because I have nothing more to say, but because I am dizzy again.

"Are you the Serpentin who tried to kill Diamond last night?" she questions distrustfully, standing as far from me as possible.

"I am half-Illumaen and half-Serpentin. I didn't try to eat her, I tried to get away as she begged to be eaten."

"Ha! Like that actually happened!" she flips her gleaming magenta hair arrogantly.

"I can hardly believe it myself. I've had a long night, I would appreciate if you did not mock me," I glare at her with a deadpan expression. The Illumaen method of problem-solving is simply to be straight with people.

"Hahaha, you Illumaens... Serpentins... Foreigners; you are so hilarious," she giggles infuriatingly. Just like Diamond. Are they all this flippant?

I feel frustration and anger bubbling up within me, so I employ the Serpentin defence mechanism. I maintain eye contact with her, running my fingers across my upper torso, flicking my tongue over my lips. She makes a hasty retreat back to her corner of the elevator, remaining there until the doors open and I leave.

"My apologies, only you goaded me so," I crack a smile as the doors close in front of her stunned face. That likely did not aid my damage control plan, but my head is not able to cope with Electrolans for any length of time.

About to swing into the conference room, I stop in my tracks. The wall and door are glass, so I can see straight into the room. The glass has a tint which can be darkened to provide privacy, but that is only activated once the door is locked and the meeting starts. Two Scytharians are there, conversing with the Electrolan delegation in a remarkably casual fashion. I spot Diamond cornering one, hands on hips, while the other speaks confidently to the male section of the group. Pushing the door open silently, I glide into the room, catching some snippets of conversation.

"Make a deal with the Illumaens? This is why you came here? I wouldn't trust that diplomat as far as I could throw her!" That is, of course, Diamond speaking.

"She has been calm and civil with us previously. We tried to assassinate her, twice, and she remained level-headed. Though we prize military prowess and suitably focused anger, she possesses a quality of strength and peace we admire."

"Absolute nonsense! In a fit of weakness, she almost digested me last night! She is partially Serpentin."

"We are aware of that fact…"

"And still you insist on meeting her? I would imagine that she is unable to attend talks today. I sedated her with a potent drug in self-defence."

"Rubbish - Never heard so much of it in one utterance before," I chip in, as "level-headed" and "calm" as ever. The only external evidence of my frustration is the empty bottle in my hand, which I crush before pitching it into the bin.

"You… How did you manage to exit your room, let alone get up here?" Diamond bursts, her gestures all jagged and violent.

"As aforementioned, I am half-Serpentin. You have no experience in formulating drugs targeted at them. You designed that sedative to have nasty side effects on an Illumaen, forgetting that it is only half as effective on me. It was not administered in self-defence - my cognitive functions were impaired the moment I entered that room with you."

"See - she is a liar on top of all those flaws!" she spits furiously.

"Will you allow us a moment?" the Scytharian who was speaking to the men cuts across her measuredly. That is the politest Scytharian I have ever seen.

"Ugh, fine, have it your way. Trust me, you won't get anywhere with her."

"Well, we do not trust you, so I guess we can just ignore you," the other jibes.
Diamond sighs dramatically, and waves her entourage out of the room, slamming the door behind her so that it shivers on its hinges.

"Sit, please," I nod pleasantly to the Scytharians, using the dial on one of the opaque side walls to increase the tint level on the glass wall and door. With a little difficulty, they balance on the chairs, their feet not quite reaching the floor.

"I am sorry about the unforgiving furniture. We have chair legs with adjustable heights on Illuma."

"We will put up with the discomfort to consult with you. I am Satriolo, and this is my comrade Ghiski."

"It is a pleasure to meet you both," I smile in Scythaon. Their faces light up, and they relax a little. I try to conceal my suspicion. We are, after all, at war.

"In truth, we are mostly just glad that the annoying woman with the long hair has left."

"I concur with that."

"Did you really eat her?"

"Regretfully, no. She is exceptionally irritating."

"Hmm…" Satriolo muses in concurrence. "Anyway, let's focus on business matters. We come to you as the Ambassador for Illuma. By extension, you represent the Illumaen Union."

"Yes?" Awaiting the punchline, I sit very still, bemused.

"We have intelligence regarding an impending threat to the Union."

"Is this the threat from Scythaon? If so, bear in mind that Illuma is cognisant of your quarrel with us."

"No, we are putting our differences with you aside to convey this information, don't you see?"

"I see that you both demonstrated great courage in coming here." It is always best to flatter the Scytharians, they respond beautifully.

"Well thank you, Ambassador," Ghiski grins bashfully, earning an appropriate glare from Satriolo.

"Back to the task at hand," Satriolo continues, clearing his throat to indicate that he means to continue his oration. "The threat, Jade, is from the Serpentin Empire. I have spoken to some friends who have acquaintances within the Serpentin military. They intend to pick off the weaker planets first, and then tackle Illuma and Prometheus while their inhabitants are distracted by the fragmentation of everything around them. We came here to warn the Electrolans that they would certainly be the first to go if they separated from the Union."

"And I got in the way - I apologise profusely for that."

"Oh no, it is perfect! We could only have dreamed of an Illumaen diplomat happening to be here. We couldn't exactly arrive at Illuma to speak with you, there is an ongoing feud between our species."

"Well, in truth I had no idea that the Serpentins were planning this."

"But you rule the Serpentins, surely you knew!" Ghiski interjects, silenced swiftly by Satriolo's glare.

"I sadly have insubordinate generals, and a *Tradition Keeper* who tirelessly fights to get her way, in the name of keeping the Empire pure," I glance kindly at Ghiski.

"The Electrolans have refused our counsel. They say that they are making a deal with the Serpentins. There is one, Nada, here at the moment, yes?" Satriolo retakes the role of spokesman.

"Yes... she apparently only came to irk me... Turns out she is more facetious than I initially concluded..."

"I don't actually believe their claims. Did you see the hate in Diamond's eyes talking about Serpentins?" Ghiski re-joins the discussion.

"I did, but Diamond, I have decided, is a skilled actress. She can laugh, cry, flirt, rage and act all shy on cue," I turn to look over my shoulder, sensing that Diamond is on the other side of the subterfuge, plotting with Nada, somehow. If Nada would not stoop to learn Electrolan, then Diamond could have learned Serpentin.

"I wouldn't trust a Serpentin as far as I can throw them - apologies Jade," Ghiski's eyes dart about as he speaks, revealing his Scytharian distrust of everyone and everything, a striking feature of each converging of Scytharians with another race.

"Well, I wouldn't either Ghiski," I laugh, relieving some of the pent-up tension weaving itself through the room.

"If Nada is indeed here to forge an alliance with the Electrolans, the terms will be extremely one-sided," he comments.
"From here, it is not difficult to infiltrate the rest of the Union..."
I drift off into pensive silence, and it takes Satriolo to bring me back. He leaves a respectful minute for me to gather my thoughts.

"So, er, what are we going to do about this?" he queries.
"I have not the faintest idea, in all honesty."

"Great. You said that she'd instantly know exactly what the plan of action would be," Ghiski whines pathetically.

"Ghiski!" I snap sternly, and he sinks further into the seat that is already dwarfing his stout frame. My head is pounding.

"Ghiski, I will do some investigating this afternoon, and then this evening you and Satriolo will convene with me in my room. Agreed?"

"Agreed," Satriolo affirms, glaring with irritation at Ghiski.

"We can compare notes."

"Good idea."

"So, shall we say 15:00?"

"Okay."

"Excellent. Now, I am heading to the canteen, then to locate both Diamond and Nada. Until this evening, good day."

We stand in unison, despite the pair of Scytharians having to jump down from their perches. I spin around on my heels and stride away, thrusting the door into the glass partition to my right as I swing around towards the elevator. No Electrolans. Where are those pesky walking batteries when you need them? Uhh... I guess that I will just have to tackle the stairs. One, two, three, five, twenty, four... Wait, what? Eimear better get that sample to Illuma, I need to know if this drug has any permanent effects. Barely managing one flight, I slide down the next, head in hands.

With much exertion, and many episodes of face-planting into banisters or the floor, I make it as far as the canteen. I really hope my face doesn't look like I got into a serious fight. My head is pounding, and my stomach is screaming at me to feed it. I strive to walk normally, stumbling towards the buffet. Swiping a plate, I gather numerous fruits and vegetables (essentially anything with a decent water content), and wobble over to a table beside the window, as per usual. Easing myself into the seat, I sit up, taking a sip of water before eating...

Oh goodness. Not now. Please, just, go away. Leave me in peace. Do not notice me, have mercy! I do a double-take, praying that what I see is gone when I look in front of me again. Alas, the tragic scene remains. Nada and Diamond are sitting literally a metre away from me. Well, at least I know that Diamond's flirtatious demeanour is nothing personal. She is trying way too hard to psychologically disarm Nada. Nada is having none of it, and it shows. Nada was never one to disguise her feelings. Impaling a piece of apple-like fruit on my fork, I nibble it slowly, enjoying the show. I could get inside Diamond's mind, but she would sense an intrusion. All I can do is eat quietly and study their body language. Diamond clearly has the opinion that she is owning the negotiation. This should ameliorate my reputation rescue. I'd imagine that someone who was almost eaten yesterday wouldn't go and hang out with another dangerous Serpentin the next morning. Just a thought.

Diamond leans forward, playing with her hair - all things she does when backing me into a corner. Nada, on the other hand, is staring dispassionately at her, with a subtle, incredulous raising of her eyebrows. I can only see Nada's face, so I watch her lips.

They are conversing in Serpentin. I am amazed that Nada has not yelled at Diamond in Serpentin before now. They, it seems, were reluctantly cooperating to produce a ruse. Nada is saying something relating to an agreement, contract... a treaty of some sort? Wow, lying is a bold manoeuvre in company with Diamond. Sometimes it felt like she could see straight through me while we were negotiating. Diamond is writing on some paper... Is that what I think it is?? I can't believe it! I'm going to kill Nada when I next speak to her.

    "Hey Jade, what'ya doing?" Electra almost sends me into cardiac arrest.
    "Sssh, sit Electra," I hiss in a panicked whisper. She looks at me in bewilderment, before obeying.
    "What is it?" she whispers loudly back.
Is there a volume control on her? If so, she needs to dial it down.

"Nada and Diamond are forming an alliance or pact. I need to know what is involved.

"Why?"

"I am the Empress of Serpentin. My title is Hydra. I am supposed to be running the Serpentin Empire. I hate being left out of the loop."

"Oh."

She finally falls silent, evidently processing my rank and power. I re-focus on the dissenting females before us. That was quick - Nada has the pen. Diamond is fighting for possession of it. The Pen of Destiny. It is aptly dubbed, for one term written in that agreement could well be the difference between prosperity and poverty, life and death. I speak solely on behalf the Electrolans, of course. Nada always gets what she wants. Diamond slams her plate on the table, standing with a jolt. Plucking her dish from the table, she struts away, leaving Nada with the Pen of Destiny and the paper. Nada breathes a sigh of relief. Until, that is, she glances over and notices me giving her a death glare. I beckon her over, maintaining the stern look as she abandons her empty plate and trudges over.

"What? I was going to tell you all about it."

"Is that before or after you form a pact with them?"

"Is it appropriate to discuss this with that present?" she points disapprovingly at Electra.

Electra flashes a cheesy grin, before vanishing remarkably stealthily.

"I am not to be mocked, nor are you to ever go behind my back again. I must be included in all foreign affairs, Nada. Or else..."

"Sweetie, you wouldn't. You haven't the guts."

"You have some nerve. I'll strangle you with your own guts if you persist. And, my title is Hydra, not Sweetie," I snarl at her, finishing my lunch and storming up to my room. My headache is fading slightly, but not my astonishment at this state of affairs.

Closing the door ever so softly, I toss my jacket on the chair beside the mirror and sit heavily on the bed. Tapping into the Illumaen line through my earpiece, I am at last able to converse with civilisation.

"How are the negotiations faring Jade?"

"They are progressively worsening with every passing hour."

"We expected some resistance. Those simple people cannot comprehend our logical reasons for the Union."

"They are not simple."

"Simpler than us. That makes them lower than us."

"You know, I thought that Illumaens were above partiality."

"It is not a matter of partiality. They are rather stupid. Have you not observed them, assuming they know everything?"

"I have observed their slight deficit in rational thinking, but they have an amazing intuition and emotional intelligence."

"Pfft," the official on the other end of the line scoffs.

I have had quite enough of this. I disconnect myself without any further sound, utterly fed up with this. That was not civilisation I just heard. That was bigotry and snobbery. I hate it. I am surrounded by it. Yet, somewhere deep inside, I agree with it. My surface indignation is countered by a deep-seated pride of self, an assuredness of superiority which repulses me.

It was exactly the same when I was growing up on Earth. I was chastised for being different. By different, I meant my height and my choice of conversation, mostly concerning science and other educational matters. I had the intellectual edge, so they never understood my topics of conversation. I loved literature and drama. I was a real history buff too. Ah yes, history - well, they had a host of names for me relating to that. When we studied the Cold War, I was renamed a Communist. When we studied World War Two and Hitler, I was a Nazi. One boy said it to my face, so I looked him dead in the eye and asked:

"How on earth could I be a Communist Nazi."

I continued to death-stare him as his expression turned from cocky to dumbfounded. Haha, good times. Now, my whole life is a drama, so crazy that, as Aunt Skifa would say: "You couldn't make it up." While planets around here are generally united, they fight each other over the pettiest dissensions, and I guess I can say that the Galaxy is embroiled in one big Cold War. It would take very little to toss us into chaos.

Oh, how I wish that Chromium was here. I mourned for the month after his death, mostly mourning the loss of such potential and intellect. I, after all, only knew him for the briefest period of time. Now, I am reminded of his heart and gentleness when I stare into the sheen of my pendant. Not without emotion, but I no longer fear tears escaping my eyes. I suppose that I have accepted his demise. Nonetheless, he was a beacon of surety and logic in this bizarre and paradoxical universe. I shall perpetually miss that aspect of his existence.

Taking out a small vial of Peppermint essential oil, I rub it on my temples, inhaling the reviving scent. I wipe the residue off around my navel. Peppermint aids digestion. Unfortunately, it also sends me dashing to the toilet two minutes later. I am drying my hands when I hear noises in my room. Tiptoeing out, praying that the door is well-oiled, I survey the scene. Seemingly nobody. Padding across the carpet, I stop at the foot of my bed.

All of a sudden, Electra jumps out at me, electrocuting me. I leap out of my skin, quickly adapting to laugh at the prank. Eimear peeks out from behind her bed.
    "What are you two up to? Mischief no doubt."
    "Just having some fun," Eimear grins deceitfully.
    "We are planning a prank on Nada."
    "You weren't supposed to tell her!" Eimear springs to life, exasperated by Electra.
    "Huh, a prank?"
    "Yep, I can't wait!" Electra squeals.

"Do you want to live to become the Electron Flow Regulator?"

"Of course."

"Then, do not irritate Nada. You'll find yourself in a tight spot otherwise."

Electra stares up at me, momentarily tongue-tied, when the silence is shattered by Eimear sneezing. Oops... she has a reaction akin to hay fever when she smells Peppermint.

"Oh no, I apologise profusely Eimear!"

"It's fine," she sniffs.

"We met Diamond and Nada on the way to Nada's room when we were coming up here," Electra chirps.

"It looks serious," Eimear chips in. "They were debating some contract."

"An alliance or peace pact probably," I cringe, sickened at the concept of Nada forming a "peaceful" bond.

"Nada? Never! It has to be a ruse," Eimear's brows knit together with concern.

"I know. It is my impression that they have already decided much. Nada will doubtless try to weave some deadly clause into the documentation."

"You mean like the Firstborn Clause?"

"Ah yes, the Firstborn Clause, the cruellest one."

"I am the Firstborn child of my household," Electra pipes up again, all too enthusiastically. "What is a clause anyway?"

"A clause is a condition in a contract. It is usually very important. The Firstborn clause we are talking about is a condition that the planet in alliance with Serpentin must provide every firstborn child as a servant to us."

"For how long?"

"However long they stay alive."

"That's just crazy! I have a vital role to play here. You'd never be able to take me away."

"That is precisely why we need to sabotage or block this agreement."

All of a sudden, I acquire the most wondrous idea.

"Electra, are you able to distract Diamond away from Nada?"

"I could ask her to help me with educational work I need to finish."

"Great. Eimear, if Nada looks like she is going to insist on Diamond's remaining with her, you step in and tell her that I need to meet with her."

"I can do that."

"Excellent. No pranks, understood?"

"Yes Jade," they grin cheekily in unison. They are a right pair. Eimear has to be at least twenty-five in Earth terms, but she is transformed back into a child again when in the presence of Electra. It is quite delightful to see her transformation from brooding and apathetic to sunny and playful.

Now to enact my side of the bargain. Jogging down the stairs, I soon arrive at the foyer.

Saving Face

I scan the oceanic volume of people, searching for an indication of the Scytharians I met with earlier. That meeting needs to be moved forward to now. Right now. Spying Satriolo's head bobbing among the shoulders of the crowd, I shimmy and squeeze my way through the throng. I cannot comprehend why there is perpetually such a choking density of bodies here. The perfect place, admittedly, for illicit meetings and less than above board deals to be struck. And yet it all appears so innocent and upbeat... Unlike the streets on Serpentin, where you are just as likely to witness a murder as, for example, seeing a romantic kiss under the Eiffel Tower on Earth.

Snaking closer to the pair, I assess them. Good, they are not fraternising with any in the bait ball. Yes, that is a marvellous metaphor. A huge bait ball of hominoids, and some not so human-like, milling around. I almost step on a creature not dissimilar to an oversized iguana wearing a tie, who is evidently having a heated discussion with... a bird of some description. Or what a human would classify as a bird.

"A word in private Satriolo, Ghiski," I whisper fiercely.
"Yes Jade. Where?"
"The conference rooms are free."
"They are on the top floor. The steps are laborious."
"Grab an Electrolan then. Let's go!"
Cornering an unsuspecting resident, we politely request transport in the elevator. They flat refuse. Ghiski tries the tactic of 'we will annihilate your family if you do not help us.' Unsurprisingly, the Electrolan is not phased. The two men look confidently at me. Following some consideration, I attempt to reason with them. The young man snorts with disbelief, looking down his nose at us with disgust. Although, he has to look up to see me.

The piercing eyes still burn into me. 'Fine, I have one other option,' I sigh.

"Do you know Diamond young man?"

"Yes, everybody knows Diamond."

"How is she after the unfortunate incident?"

"She got out alive."

"So, boy, would you be able to escape something like that?" I stroke my bottom lip with my first two fingers.

"No, I probably wouldn't stand a chance."

"In that case, I suggest you help us, because if you do not, either I will eat you, or some other Serpentin will, after Diamond has sold you all into slavery."

"What authority do you possess to threaten me?" he raises his voice.

"I am the Hydra of Serpentin, trying to help you poor little otherwise-slaves. A glimmer of reciprocation would be appreciated."

"Ugh, fine!" he huffs, persisting in his incredulity, marching brusquely towards the lift.

"I express my utmost gratitude, kind young man," I smile coyly.

Once upstairs, I usher them into a conference room, shooing the Electrolan back into the lift to hasten his departure from earshot. Hurriedly tinting the glass walls, I remain standing.

"What is so urgent? We were gathering intelligence," Satriolo sighs with disapproval.

"I have my own intelligence, and it is imperative that we act swiftly, and with discretion."

"What's happening?" Ghiski, as usual, assumes the densest role in the room, much to the ire of Satriolo.

"What is your plan then, Hydra, Jade?" Satriolo pushes through.

"I plan to go in and fix it."

"How, may I ask?"

"I will speak to both parties and convince Diamond of her idiocy. Encourage her to burn the contract or shred it."

"Contract?!"

"She and Nada are drawing one up to outline the terms of their alliance."

"Have you caught a glimpse of it?"

"No, although I am familiar with Nada's diplomacy, or lack thereof. She will unfailingly insert a clause or condition which disarms Electrolaia, cripples their economy, and almost certainly halves their population."

"I understand the rush to halt the discussion now," Satriolo acknowledges, his brow furrowed with concern.

"Backup is necessary. Will you two linger outside the room while I go in and handle the state of affairs?"

"Absolutely. We are well equipped for armed support."

"Can you stun as an alternative to killing?"

"We have self-defence training, sufficient to knock out a Serpentin. I cannot be sure that it will work on an Electrolan."

"The back-up is for the Serpentin, not the Electrolan. I have already concocted a plot to separate the parties temporarily. If I can get either alone, I have a reasonable chance of succeeding."

"That seems to be an acceptable course of action. What is the distraction?"

"My servant, Eimear, and an Electrolan friend of hers, Electra, are going to draw the two away from each other."

"Electra? The Electra??" Ghiski chips in.

"Yes, one of the most powerful Electrolans on the planet. The prodigy."

"Wow," he breathes, stunned and dazzled.

"So, let me get this straight Jade - you have endangered the wellbeing of the heir to the most vital job on Electrolaia..."

"Yes, Satriolo. Indeed, I have. If it all goes south, it will be her own fault. I gave her specific instructions not to pose a threat to Nada. My servant will bear the brunt of the responsibility. I am to meet Nada presently in my quarters, where Eimear will have led her."

"South? Are they on the run??"

"Oh, apologies, I used an Earth expression. It means things going wrong."

"Ah, I see."

"Time is of the essence; I will depart from you. Follow at a discreet distance. I will take the stairs down to my quarters."

"Understood."

Affirming that nobody is stalking me, I saunter down the stairs, relatively relaxed. I have confidence in Eimear's abilities to deal with any matter I entrust to her. She truly is a faithful servant. Knocking non-aggressively, I open the door in a snail-like fashion. I expect to be faced with Nada, tapping her hip, glaring at me. But no angered Serpentin greets me. Only an emptiness, and a deathly silence. I nose around, anticipating Electra jumping out at me at any moment. Nobody. Not a soul. I should know, I am a telepath. I can sense presences.

'What if something has gone wrong?' I fret. I speed out of my room, and down to Nada's. Waving to Satriolo and Ghiski, I beckon them to accompany me. Pressing my ear against the door, I strain to catch a conversation. Nothing. Correction - almost nothing... A faint growling, and a kind of terrified whimpering. She's done it again.

Busting the door open, I am the one in a stance, tapping my hip, glaring at Nada. She hardly notices. The first thing I observe is her fingertips brushing her belly. It's empty, thank goodness. Her other hand is pressed against the wall, with a young neck in its grip. The victim's flailing hands drop, and she slides down the wall, going limp.

"Finally, now you won't electrocute me while I get you down my neck," Nada flashes her teeth. They are pristinely white, which is not a total shock. After all, she rarely bothers to utilise them. She just gulps her meals down, not even bothering to taste her food.

"Nada!" I bellow, making for her. Hooking my foot on something, I fall flat. It is an unconscious Diamond, with a mark on her jugular where Nada has pinched her blood vessels, causing her to faint.

"Nada, stop what you are doing RIGHT NOW!" I bark. I got here just a little too late. Nada, using the wall to prop Electra up, is feeding her feet into her maw. Words are getting me nowhere. Marching over to them, I slap Nada on the cheek. She pushes me away, slipping her victim's knees into her throat. I cannot hit her on the jaw, she could bite Electra's legs off with one chomp. So instead, I push her hard while holding Electra up. She staggers backwards, spluttering and spitting the girl's feet out.

"What in the Empire are you doing?!" I yell at her, laying Electra on her side on the floor, before marching over and sitting Nada on the bed. She glares defiantly at me.

"Diamond signed the contract," she states coldly.

"What contract?!"

A generalised gesture guides my gaze to a piece of paper, sitting lonely near the head of the bed. It is only then that I notice Eimear passed out nearby, her head obviously having struck the tiled floor of the bathroom. I must have moved her legs away from my path when I opened the door. Dashing over to check if she is okay, I direct Ghiski to watch her.

"You brought the bite-sized warriors too? Seriously??"

"I warned you. No leaving me out of crucial pacts, alliances or takeovers. I have a mind to demote you."

"You can't. I know the law inside out."

"Well, I happen to also. I recall that insubordination is severely punished."

"Haha, as I mentioned before, you wouldn't have the guts."

"Oh, really..." I snarl, stalking over to her. "You have bullied, disobeyed and disrespected me for quite long enough. I have had it with you."

"Well, I think you are overreacting. I managed to get Diamond to sign away every firstborn child to us. That is a great stride for the Empire," her pace quickens, attempting to talk herself out of the wrong.

"No, no it isn't. Stand before your Hydra!"

Nada eases herself to her feet, tentatively. She is nervous. Very nervous. Terribly nervous. Finally, I have found a raw nerve I can put pressure on.

"Satriolo, can you come over here please?" I flash a big, intimidating smile at Nada, who, rather oddly, does not stare back for once.

"Hold her down!"

He catches her from behind, twisting her arms behind her back. She curses at me, at him, at everything, fidgeting and twisting to free herself.

"This is for calling me bite-sized," he winds a wire around her wrists, which cuts into her when she tries to wriggle free.

"Just a moment, I'd like to leave you marinate in your fear for a little while," I laugh.

I walk over to check on Eimear. She is coming around, muttering to herself in her native language, before adjusting and speaking Serpentin to me.

"Hey, how are you feeling?" I ask.

"My head hurts."

"You don't need to rush; I have everything sorted," I soothe.

Ambling back to Nada, who is sitting on her bed, I note that she is whiter than usual. Ghiski asks how he can help further, so I assign him and Satriolo to attend to Electra, who is still disoriented. I smile at the macho warriors stooping to help her, the daylight reflecting off their dark, shiny, bald heads. Most Scytharians are tanned, but these two are a darker shade than most. Right, focus. Back to the task at hand. Asking Eimear to stand between me and the men, I chuck my jacket on the chair behind me, scoring a perfect landing so that it drapes neatly. Unbuttoning my shirt, I leave it hanging open, showing my torso to Nada. This is practically the power move to end all power moves in Serpentin culture. Nada bites her nails when she is bored or anxious. The unavailability of her hands is driving her nuts. She squirms and bites her lip, extremely uncomfortable. She knows how this is going to end.

"Is there anything you want to say?"
"I offer my servant in my stead."
"Not a good enough trade."
"Please?"
Wow, that sounded painful. Please, resonating from the vocal cords of Nada. I could almost fall over with the shock of it.
"Say that you are sorry, and that you will step down."
"No! I was born to do this job."
"Hmm... Which job? *Tradition Keeper,* or my next meal? I consider the latter to be the most suitable for you."
"Come on, just let me go, and I will always consult you in the future." She has the nerve to be insincere, even now.
"No. The law is the law. I charge you with acting against the interests of the Empire, treason, and any other description of your reprehensible actions."
"I wouldn't go that far," she looks at the floor like a scolded puppy. The difference is that I would not eat a dog. They are too cute.

Casting her stilettos aside, I grab a washcloth from the bathroom. Untying her, I offer the cloth to her.
"Clean your feet, and preferably take your trousers off." I cautiously unwind the wire on her wrists, wary of a kick or punch.
 Her eyes narrowing suspiciously, she obeys, before sitting back down.
"Thank you."
Stroking my stomach, I look quietly at her, as she shifts in her position.
"Give me your hand Nada."
Putting her hand out, she rolls her eyes.
"What, are you going to slap me on the wrist or something?"
"Quit the attitude!" Taking her hand, I place it flat against my abdomen, just above the navel. She flinches, twitching away from me. I hold it there, allowing her to feel my stomach's empty rumblings.

"What exactly is your point?!" she snaps, recoiling, clearly afraid.

"That, my dear, is where you are going. I thought you might want to know what it feels like from the outside first."

"Don't be stupid, I know what an empty stomach feels like. I have experienced it, you know."

"Ah, yes. But not the inside of a full stomach though."

"Well, no…"

"Do not fret. You will know what that feels like very soon."

"Seriously, no, please!" her pitch skyrockets to a yelp, and that agonising word leaves her lips for the second time ever.

Flailing and kicking, she attempts to get away from me. I simply get a firm grip on her calves and hold them stationary. I am a lot stronger than I look.

"I guess you will now know how your victims felt, before they perished," I smile with vindictive triumph, before popping my jaw open.

Eimear sidles up to help, and I point at Nada's shoulders. Eimear pins her to the bed, dodging the torrent of unmentionable swearing and insults pouring from her mouth, and her flapping arms. Once I reach her fairly wide hips, some of her legs and feet are in my expanding belly. Realising this, she begins to kick, and wriggle, and protest vigorously. I have never before had so much trouble with prey fighting me. Boy, has she got some power in those legs. She twists around, still shouting and roaring at me. I have very sensitive ears, so after some time I put my hand over her mouth to muffle the din. Eventually, I feel her shoulders and head drop into my cavernous stomach.

Eimear scurries off to get a towel, as it would seem that I am drooling everywhere. Most inelegant. Electra stands up, seemingly recovered. The trio turn to find me squashed against the foot of the bed, relying on the support to continue breathing.

"Yikes…" Ghiski remarks, cringing as he speaks.

"Yes, I know, I probably, look, grotesque…" I pant, hands supporting my disproportionate gut from underneath.

"My dear, do you need assistance?" Satriolo steps in, offering a hand.

"Much, appreciated," I end up digging my nails into his palm as I haul myself up. Grimacing, he takes it like a man. Eimear starts to wipe my mouth, but I wave her away, finishing the task myself.

"Huh?" Diamond has just come to, and the first view she receives is of me sitting, striving for breath, stomach resting in my lap.

"Where's Electra? What did you do with her?" she sits up, glaring distrustfully at me.

"I am here, Diamond. It is Nada who is in residence," she holds back from giggling as she points to me.

"Nada… she made me sign a contract…"

"Contract, what contract?"

"The one between Electrolaia and Serpentin."

"It's over there. Burn it, shred it, crush it to a pulp, eat it, whatever. I never saw it, never read its contents, and certainly never caught sight of the two signatures making it legally binding. Destroy it Diamond, destroy it," I crack an insipid smile, before dragging oxygen into my restricted lungs again.

"I want, to go, to my room, Eimear," I tug at her sleeve.

"Of course, Hydra, most exalted one. You must recuperate, and above all, take pleasure in your meal."

"Hmm, yes… Tell me what transpired before I reached you in the morning, when my prey is not so deliciously active. Good day."

It is only early in the evening, so when I reach my room, I inform Eimear that she can go and socialise in the canteen if she wishes. She takes the hint and leaves me promptly. The Electrolans measure the hours from the time when the sun sets, so it is still light. They usually go to sleep at 00:00.

"Hmmm… you were one stubborn package of nourishment, Nada."

A sharp kick challenges my opinion, along with an unmistakeable change of posture and a prolonged gurgle from my contented insides.

"Ugh, Nada, you do realise that scratching has no negative impact, rather resulting in a decidedly pleasant caressing of my stomach walls..." Despite her stature being slightly shorter than mine, she weighs more than me, so I struggle to maintain command of her as she thrashes around and jiggles my digestive tract until I am sure my second brain is dazed.

Later on, in the evening, I am dozing, my fingertips dancing over my stretched torso, when Eimear returns along with Diamond.

"How is your dinner behaving?" she grins, not bothering to hide her glee at Nada getting what was coming to her.

"Haha... she's a fighter, I'll give her that," I smile affectionately at my stomach.

"Oh, goodness, that is still a jarring sight!" Diamond blurts upon seeing me.

"Diamond, will you now fix the holes you punched in my reputation? I have, after all, saved your planet from enslavement and death."

"Since you saved me from my terrible misjudgement signing that paper, I have come to view you in a slightly more positive light. I have explained the accurate account to as many people as possible, to repair the damage to your reputation."

"Good to know, in case I have to negotiate or do business with you in the future. I was thinking that I would have to resuscitate my own reputation after that debacle - thank you for giving me one less thing to do."

"When are you going to free her?" Diamond asks curiously.

"I was not planning to free her, unless you mean when..."

"No, spare me details, please. I was stupid to want that end for myself. Absurd. I sense that she is in so much distress, that I just want the pain to stop."

"Diamond, I shall tell you my plan. I will sleep on it, and decide in the morning. Nada deserves the most severe punishment. I do not think that you know her very well. I know, that since I met her, she has consumed at least six servants, and two romantic partners. Think of it as saving many by killing one."

"Aren't all Serpentins like that?"

"No, Nada is especially voracious. I have had Eimear as my servant for a whole month. Granted, I am half-Illumaen, so I do not see the point in dining on people weekly."

Nada turns, making me giggle. It tickles quite a lot. I palpate my abdomen, kneading it to see the state of her. Hmm, she needs a bit more air to breathe. I gulp some air down, to buy me a little more deciding time.

"I am tired Diamond, would you please come back in the morning, with Electra?"

"Certainly, I will leave you in peace."

I breathe a sigh of relief as I hear the door click shut. Eimear assists in straightening my bedsheets and adjusting my pillow so that I can fall asleep comfortably.

"Thank you, goodnight."

"Is there anything I can do?"

"Maybe... stroking my belly until I fall asleep?"

"Sure, like this?"

"Yes, that's good..." I muse as my eyes flutter closed, the rhythm of my digestion, and my servant helping it along, lulling me to sleep.

Judgements from on High

I am yanked from sleep very early in the morning by a desperate scrabbling.

"Nada, what are you trying to achieve?" I groan sleepily. She responds by kicking violently and doing somersaults inside me.

"Nada, stop. That is not going to ameliorate your plight." In the dim light, I recognise why she is panicking. Before, my torso moved in a jerky, abrupt fashion, indicating something moving inside the stretchy, dry cavity. However, the motion has altered to a rippling effect. There is a lot of fluid in there. She is drowning. If I can funnel some more air to her, she will live until I wake again.

"Nada, stop writhing around and listen for once. If you keep this up, you will lose your air supply. You are going to make me… burp!" My eructation startles Eimear, who jolts upright and starts muttering, almost praying, in Xenonian.

"Oh, you stupid woman Nada. No, I will not give you another chance!" I stretch out as my stomach growls and rumbles. A strange bubbling sound accompanies Nada suffocating. The satisfaction washes over me, and I smile contentedly to myself as I curl up and go back to sleep.

I stir to the sound of Eimear communicating with my earpiece, which she has stealthily removed.

"Who is it?" I ask groggily.

"Illuma. They are calling a meeting of the council."

"Why? Do I have to go??"

"It is concerning Electrolaia's status in the Union. They have requested your presence in a few hours."

"Thank you."
I wait patiently for Eimear to cease the conversation, before yawning loudly.

"I do not feel like going to a meeting today. What will the rest of the Society think of me if I walk in looking like this?" I slap my distended abdomen. I look like I am carrying a full-term baby. In spite of this, it is much improved from the state of me last night.

"Diamond is coming back to see if you showed mercy to Nada. Have you decided?"

"Nada sealed her own fate. I was going to give her more air, but she did not listen. She ended up drowning. It was her own fault. She kept wriggling around and giving me indigestion."

"Right, okay, I can see that..." Eimear cringes, willing me to cease my description.

"I never put you down as the squeamish type Eimear," I laugh, disconcerting her further.
She is about to lock herself in the bathroom when a rapid succession of knocks announces Electra's arrival. Just when I was going to get up...

"Oh, no! Eimear, get me something decent to wear, quick!"

"No time, get back in bed. Here, cover up with the duvet!"
I prop myself up just in time for Electra to come bounding over, as rambunctious as ever.

"Now I get to tell you all about our prank!" She shrieks, and I cover my ears.

"I am absolutely looking forward to your epic tale, but could you possibly turn the volume down on your voice?"

"Yes, sorry."

"Great. Continue..."

"So, I told Eimear my master plan while we were on our way to Nada's room. She didn't find it that funny."

"I told you not to do it!"

"Spoil sport! She saw the amusing side during the event though."

"Yeah, for a fleeting moment before I was floored."

"So anyway," she continues, "I went into Nada's room, and stood behind the door, where I would be hidden when she opened the door. I heard Nada and Diamond talking to Eimear, so I grabbed my chance. I took hold of the door handle, and channelled some electricity into it, keeping it flowing with one finger while I waited for Nada to open it. You should have heard her yelp when she touched the metal! It was hilarious!"

"She did jump quite far. Admittedly, it was mirth worthy." I take pride in the fact that Eimear sounds so very Illumaen.

"She opened the door, shoving it very forcefully, squishing me onto the wall. I still had room to reach around and catch her on the wrist. She totally thought that Diamond did it. Diamond and Nada started scrapping, during which I got Nada in the small of her back. Only this time I got caught. I couldn't avoid giggling. Eimear had snuck in behind me, so when Nada lunged at me, I dodged her and she hit Eimear instead. That's why she hit her head on the bathroom floor."

"Yeah, thanks for that," Eimear rubs the sore spot gingerly.

"Nada was really, really furious. She attacked Diamond next, doing some weird neck pinch that made her drop unconscious. I was completely alone in the room with a raging maniac. She flung me against the wall, holding my neck in a pincer grip. I zapped her again, and she said that she would rip me limb from limb right there. Then, all of a sudden, she freakishly calmed down. She obviously had had an idea. Her scowl morphed into an unnerving smirk, and she began running her fingers across her stomach."

"She was preparing to eat you Electra."

"Well, I didn't think about that at the time - she was strangling me. I passed out. I don't remember anything until I awoke to two concerned Scytharians looking down at me."

"That is quite the adventure, you two."

"Do you think Nada is coming back? Did you spit her out yet??" Electra's eyes dart about anxiously.

"No, there's zero chance of that happening. I dealt with her."

"Ooh, how? Give me details," she grins eagerly.

"No, you really do not want to hear any details Electra," I say with a tinge of self-loathing.

I am beginning to regret my impulsive decision. I feel so weak, having succumbed to my desire. Why do I feel it so intensely? It is so abhorrent to find delight in another's demise. Why did I have to be born this way, so broken, so sick? When I lived on Earth, my Aunt was religious. She used to tell me about God sometimes. What would God think of all this? How angry is he with me? Could I ever ask him for forgiveness? He must be up there, shaking his head in dismay. Actually, I am "up" where I used to think God lived. Well, I guess we can't see him, so finding his domicile would be rather challenging.

All of a sudden, I notice Electra looking expectantly at me. Eimear is cocking her head, trying to work out what I am thinking. Time to intercept the silence, I guess.

"Do you want to hang out with Eimear for a couple of hours before we go back to Illuma?" I change the subject.

"Sure, sounds great!"

Eimear grimaces, but quickly softens. I think that she has grown in her affection for Electra.

"Well, if you want you can stay here with us. We will be preparing to leave, but we still have our hearing faculties if you want to chat to us."

"Cool! Yes, I can tell you about my lessons this week, I learned to do this awesome thing where I put electricity into something and it stays there..."

That ought to keep Electra entertained for hours. Her forte is talking - lots of talking! Admittedly, I do find the production of batteries on Electrolaia fascinating, so I do not mind her chattering. Eimear shields me with a towel as I waddle over to the bathroom to shower and change. All is going swimmingly until I have to put my dress on. It is stretchy, and it was always generous around the waist, hence the habit of pairing it with a belt. Unfortunately, the skirt section is not as stretchy, so I end up with the dress over my head, battling to get the lower section to my legs. Eimear loses patience faster than usual, yanking it violently over my engorged abdomen.

"Ow!" I yelp, clutching my poor stomach. Still, the dress is on, just about. There is definitely no need for a belt today.

"Right, I am just going to lie here and revise my notes, so that I have a diamond-like argument before the Society. So solid hardly anything can shatter it."

"Do you want any breakfast?" Electra asks us both out of courtesy.

"Just some water for me please Electra," I smile gently.

"Can I have some of the amazing fruit salad that's always on the buffet?" Eimear asks.

"Yes, I was going to get some for myself… We're the same Eimear!" Electra beams delightedly, believing that she has found her fruit salad soulmate.

As soon as she exits, I go back to caressing my midriff, trying to speed up the shrinking of my bold bump. It is not really something to do while someone you hardly know watches. Nada always said that I was too reserved to be a Serpentin. The Illumaens are private, mysterious people. They are not inclined to dish out their feelings, personal experiences or opinions to the general populous. Well, except for their glaring dislike of "inferior races." I really thought that they were such a remarkable, admirable people, so noble and rational. In reality, they are as bigoted as humans. They take in refugees to project a benevolent image. They give them work and lodging without a word of complaint. Yet, as soon as the huge Gothic doors close and the Council is in session, they speak of them as nothing more than livestock. They are no better than the Serpentins. Having said that, at least their actions are vastly more accommodating than the Serpentins'.

I can change Serpentin. I can pass laws, and control the government. I want to mandate education on Serpentin, that surpasses the militaristic training presently in place. Culture studies, initialisation of the arts and literature. Science. Then, gradually, ever so gradually, their attitudes can shift. Not a revolution, which invariably ends where you started. A reformation. I cannot pretend that I do not need to adjust myself. I carry within me the same inbuilt instincts as the Serpentins, and the entrenched ethos of the Illumaens.

Anyhow, for now I must remain focused on the task at hand. I pore over the papers I scribbled down, underlining and re-writing vital segments, tossing and turning on my perch to achieve the optimum writing surface while reclined on my makeshift chaise lounge, formed from the bed and a number of pillows.

All too soon, it is time to finish packing and make a move. Electra bids us farewell as we step into my personal *Jet Bubble,* compliments of the Serpentin Empire. It is astounding that, despite all the rivalries and conflict in the Galaxy, we all manage to get our civilian space transport from the same planet. It sits slap bang in the middle of the Empire, but is the only planet untouched by Serpentin soldiers or marauders. Those people won the political lottery - they produce a vehicle of such value that no one will ever destroy them. That is pure industrial and innovative power embodied. We know next to nothing about them, and their seclusion means that trade agreements are succinct, efficient, and unencumbered by political controversy. Their stance is reminiscent of Switzerland on earth. They help everyone as long as they can trade readily with them, regardless of the war and chaos around them.

I entrust Eimear with commanding the *Jet Bubble,* while I sprawl across the back seat, trying to get some rest before I reach Illuma. My brain must be operating at full capacity, which is not the case, because my stomach is constantly providing intense sensory input. I hate having that many sensitive nerve endings in my gut. I moan with relief as my stomach grumbles, reducing slightly in size.
    "Eimear, will they still notice?"

She pivots on her chair to appraise me.

"Umm, yes! You still look six months pregnant."

"Well, I guess they will just have to accept me as I am. I hope that I can digest a bit more quietly during the meeting though."

"Can't you just stop it temporarily?"

"Frankly, I have had enough of this inconvenience. I just want to be my normal size, and not to have my attention tirelessly trained on my abdomen," I snap crankily.

"Okay, okay, I'm sorry I asked…"

I am close to tears. When Nada died, her energy dropped so suddenly… I robbed her of her life force… I've turned into a monster. I deserve to die for causing a death. Back on Earth, that is what used to happen. A life for a life. Perfect justice. Why did I have to go and eat Nada? She was more trouble than she was worth. My head starts to hurt again, and I rub my temples, trying to focus again.

Alighting on the landing pad on Illuma, I step tentatively out of the *Jet Bubble,* relieved that no grand delegation greets me. Dabbing my glistening eyes, I saunter slowly over to the Council building. I need a few minutes to collect my thoughts before facing the wrath of Illuma. After all, I departed from Electrolaia leaving the inhabitants, not with an ultimatum, but with a choice: leave if they wish, and they will be free to trade with whomever they please, or stay, and have all the arrangements controlled for them. The last I heard; Diamond was considering an alliance with the Scytharians.

The council is already settled when I enter the grand conference chamber. I sit Eimear outside, with piles of books pertaining to Serpentin tradition and law.

"You know that reading these will give me night terrors?"

"Yes… But you are one of the brightest people I know. You can learn things at remarkable speeds."

"Do you need me to study anything in particular?"

"Yes, the laws surrounding the *Tradition Keeper,* and their replacement. Ceremonies, criteria, etc."

"Right, I will relay the information once you are finished here."

"Excellent."

"Good luck!"

"I do not believe in luck," I utter mutedly as I turn on my heels and stride into the waiting jaws of the Illumaen Council.

Immediately, everybody rotates to stare at me. Most of them are polite enough not to focus on my stomach, but a few gawk at me most disrespectfully. Sitting in my assigned seat, I look up to Lawrence, who is poised to chair the meeting. He looks me up and down disapprovingly. This is going to be one hellish meeting.

"I have gathered you all for this special sitting of the Society, to address the Electrolan problem, and the utilisation of a differing approach in ensuring their allegiance to the Union. What say you, Jade?"

"I say, that we should draw up a fresh agreement with them. A trade agreement between them and the Union. We should pay a fair price for their electricity, and they can pay for anything they require from the Union."

"No."

"Why? My proposal is reasonable."

"The Electrolans are a completely unreasonable people. Reason has not been effective... Unless you admit your failure as a diplomat."

"I did not fail. I unearthed exactly what they desire. They want freedom from the Union, but they want to be able to forge their own alliances and trade pathways. We can simply form a trade deal, and both parties benefit."

"They need us to govern them. They are too irrational and impulsive handle their own affairs," another across the table pipes up. He has definitely been eyeing up my position since I assumed it. "I say, that Jade Firedancer has not lived up to expectation. Her mission has failed. We must appoint a new Ambassador. Besides, she is tainted with the blood of savages."

"Your proposal is sound," my own father agrees.

I knew that the situation was dire, but not this disastrous.

"Excuse me, may I speak in my defence?" I stand. That was a mistake. My opponent uses my bloated belly as fuel for his case.

"See for yourselves... Her judgement is so obviously clouded by her Serpentin nature. She even ate somebody while on a mission for Illuma. I rest my case; she cannot be entrusted with the fate of our alliances."

"This is an honourable council. You would not cast a member out without a fair trial, would you?" I argue.

"You must leave Jade," Lawrence states measuredly, giving me another of those reprimanding glances.

"Why?" I demand.

"The council does not need to provide a reason to its guests. Your services are no longer required. Guards..."

The security unit steps down to fling me outside, but I stand gracefully, straightening my dress. I step elegantly and collectedly out of the room, chin up and looking straight ahead.

"How was your meeting Jade? It was shorter than I expected."

"I am no longer a member of the Society, Eimear. I have been swept aside in favour of somebody less... Serpentin. Those were the hinges of the argument, that I was half-Serpentin. There I was, deluded into believing that Illumaens were bigger than petty racism, but no. They would have thrown me out had I not taken my leave. Let's go."

"To your quarters as planned?"

"No, we are going to Serpentin. I cannot abide this place any longer."

Even in death, Nada has achieved precisely what she wanted. I have been cut off from Illuma, with little choice but to reside permanently on Serpentin. At least, as aforementioned, there is a glimmer of promise in changing the mind-set of the Serpentins. Time to find a new *Tradition Keeper,* to devise a method of slowing the consumption of servants on Serpentin, and shrewdly re-calibrate the moral compass of the citizens. An arduous and extensive campaign stretches before me, yet I am confident of success.

Legislative Adjustments

By the time I am safely installed in my Serpentin accommodations, I feel queasy.

"Jade, you are ashen... Do you have a fever?"

"No, I have knotting cramps."

"Like you get when you menstruate?"

"Sort of. Only, that is not the reason for my pain... There are certain side effects of being only half-Serpentin. My Illumaen half means that my intestines are longer than those of a Serpentin. They are simply not designed to handle so much food in one go. Oww..." I grimace, in a foetal position on my bed.

"You got that after Widner, didn't you?"

"Yes!" I yelp.

"Sssh, everything is going to be fine. Lie flat on your back..."

Eimear elongates me, guiding me to put my arms above my head and stretch out. She plants her hands on my torso, applying pressure until she can feel the spasms. She grits her teeth, recoiling from the unhappy movements.

"I hoped that I'd only have to do this once..." she grits her teeth as she pushes down, hard, trying to relax the cramp. I bite my tongue, the metallic taste of blood distracting me slightly.

"Stop squirming around Jade. I need to hurt you to heal you."

"Aagh, stop, Eimear!" I shriek. I hope nobody else heard that. I don't need guards to come in and restrain her. "At least render me unconscious!"

She reluctantly obeys, pressing on the nerves in my shoulder, knocking me out cold.

The next morning, I set up a space to exercise, demanding that Eimear recite the laws of Serpentin tradition while I power through every core exercise I know. Time to put the excess protein I ingested to use. After an hour, I stretch for another half hour, totally spent.

"You know the laws to an impressive degree. Well done."

"I only did what I was told."

"That information shall be invaluable today, when I go through the process of selecting a worthy person to fill Nada's role."

"Serpentin."

"Yes, a worthy Serpentin..." I wander off to the bathroom, to shower and dress for the day.

"Accompany me today Eimear, as I tour the military headquarters and greet the citizens on the streets."

"Why? You shouldn't need my help with the pain today."

"Not for that reason... Meet me outside the HQ, but first go and order some plant-based energy balls from Allaara."

"Yes, of course Hydra," she curtsies respectfully, as we are in view of the public.

By the time she returns, I have the admirals and captains lined up, along with the retained invasion parties, habitually deployed to subdue a planet from the ground.

"Over here, Eimear. Tell me, how can I better use these fine resources? By the way, a quarter seem to have gone AWOL since I was last here."

"That is not unusual Hydra. What is your idea, so that I may tell you what I think? It is not my job to suggest policies."

"I need a better slave system. I propose using this invasion party to monitor the trade deals."

"Servants - they are servants, Hydra."

"By my definition, they are slaves."

"Of course, Hydra." She will wear herself out using Hydra as every second word. "It is a sound concept. What adjustments do you propose?"

"Listen up everyone, especially you," I gesture to the female section, some of whom look suspiciously satisfied. "The current system is too cheap. We shall run out of slaves if you continue to simply buy them for fodder. I wish to double the price of a slave. If I make the price prohibitive, then you will refrain from eating one a week. I shall make it a delicacy, rather than an easy meal. A quarter of the price goes to the next of kin of the slave. Half is kept by the vendors. And a quarter will comprise of taxation. If I am to improve this planet, and make us even greater, then funds are necessary."

"What will we eat Hydra?" A woman in her early twenties strokes her torso nervously.

"You will buy food we produce here, or trade with other planets for. I will use the money in the treasuries to invest in livestock."

"What is "livestock?" It sounds like more servants..." a man in his forties chips in.

"Animals for consumption. On Earth we have many animals bred for food. They are rich in protein and fat, just what you need to thrive."

"So, essentially servants... I fail to see the difference!" one of the female captains snaps crankily. I believe that is the one who is four months pregnant. Serpentins carry unborn children for around eleven months, but they can safely induce themselves at ten months if they tire of the weight. The majority of working females, like this one, will carry out this procedure in order to return to work sooner.

"These animals differ from servants in that they do not have the mental capacity of the servants we employ. They cannot, for example, dress you, or understand the training given to our servants. They will be slaughtered before we eat them. It is kinder."

"Kinder? When did that factor? You are soft, half-bred Hydra."

"Watch your tongue Admiral, or I will remove it."

"I only meant that you require the guidance of the *Tradition Keeper*. Nada should be back in a couple of days, to appraise your ideas," he rolls his eyes disrespectfully.

"I will choose a new *Tradition Keeper*. I removed Nada from office just a day or so ago. Do you have any candidates Admiral?" I smirk at him.

"Oh... No, Hydra. May you choose well."

"I am relieved that you have no suggestions, as I already have a perfectly suited candidate. I happen to know that they have an exceptional talent for remembering the letter of the law."

"They had better not be an impure half-bred Serpentin."

"No, they are not, no need to fret Admiral. That is all for now, be sure to attend my speech in a few days to announce the legislative adjustments."

"Yes Hydra, we will Hydra."

I belong everywhere, and nowhere. I long to be accepted by someone, anyone whom I can respect. I feel like Chromium was the only one who ever truly accepted and respected me. Yes, he made me feel small and kind of stupid in comparison to his abilities, but he treated me with honour. Genuine honour, not this front the Illumaen Society, or the Admirals and Captains, convey. I miss him disproportionately, considering that I only knew him for three days, maybe less.

I sigh discontentedly as I trudge back over the threshold of my quarters.

"So, who is it?" Eimear cocks her head inquisitively.

"Huh?"

"The new *Tradition Keeper*?"

"I shall not reveal that as of yet. I am still weighing that decision on the scales within my mind."

"Jade?"

"Yes?"

"I am concerned. Permission to speak my mind?"

"Granted."

"You are behaving much more like an Illumaen than is your custom. I have observed you switching back and forth according to the planet you are on. It is as if you forgot to turn the Illumaen side off."

"What if I just want to be myself? A melange of the two species, with their qualities, good and bad, displayed when I want them to be. I am weary of this war between the two sides. If they can't cope with that, then tough. I have had it with the skewed morality of the Serpentins. I will reform them, if it is the only thing I do with the time I have in power."

"You must reform the system, or the system will reform you."

"Precisely. I fear that my reformation has already been set in motion."

"It is not too late Jade. You can still come back from this, I'm sure."

"Thank you for that."

"Will you not even give me a hint?"

"I have learned, that the greatest wisdom often comes from the most surprising of places. The most powerful could be ill-equipped for their role, and the lowliest the shrewdest alive. If I could advise you only once, Eimear, I would say only this. That, along with the additional caution never to look down upon those below you. They may one day hold your fate in their hands."

"That was too cryptic, I'll stop asking for fear of being further led astray," Eimear decides wisely.

The Tradition Keeper

The next evening, I hold an assembly of all military personnel. I have a brown knee-length A-line dress sewn especially for the occasion, embroidered with metallic gold thread around the waist in a wave-like pattern, framed by two gold lines to accentuate the waist band. I wear my Jade necklace, and Jade earrings to match. I swap my silver earpiece for a gold one. My is hair styled in two long plaits, which are pinned up in a low bun, one inside the other. Just royal enough to make them sit up and take note, but not so ostentatious as to alarm them. Anything as grand as my *Installation* dress is reserved for changing laws.

"Time to go Eimear," I beckon her as I step into a pair of metallic gold kitten heels.

"It is not my place to go with you. Servants are not permitted to attend the selection of a *Tradition Keeper*."

"I found a loophole. This event is doubling as a funeral for Nada. You can accompany me there."

"No, I do not want to hear a load of Serpentins bawling and sniffling about how wonderful Nada was."

"I do not believe that Serpentins sniffle that much, Eimear. I order you to come."

"Fine."

"Lose the attitude as well please. I know that you cannot help it at times, but any other mistress would have you killed for that tone."

"Yes, Hydra. I am ready to go," she rolls her eyes while faking an appeasing tone.

When I arrive in the military building, I find my audience huddled around Nada's capsule. As there is often nothing to bury in Serpentin funerals, we instead bury the deceased's most treasured possessions. For Nada, that includes the list of all her victims, her dagger, and her favourite perfume. The list alone practically fills the capsule.

"Sorry, am I late?"

"No Hydra, you are as usual perfect in your timing."
The Admiral from yesterday has set out to ingratiate himself.
"Good. Continue."

Nada's last boyfriend clears a space so that he can speak. He sobs and exhausts himself trying not to have a breakdown while reading his speech. Nada did not deserve such an affectionate partner, that much is clear. I was glaringly wrong about Serpentins not sniffling. Eventually, after a convoluted discourse that felt a million times longer than it actually was, he melts back into the crowd. I am asked to say a few words.

"Nada. She was a loyal *Tradition Keeper*, and she loved this Empire almost as much as she liked eating." A couple in the gaggle snigger, and I exhale in relief that they found the statement amusing. "I only knew her for a short while, but I know that she served my mother for twenty-five glorious years before the mantle of Hydra passed to me. She always knew exactly how to set me straight, and her role in this Empire fit her like a glove. May she be remembered along with the greatest *Tradition Keepers.*"

I would sooner forget she ever walked the planet than hero-worship her. Those with me, however, think different. The clapping echoes off the walls as if there were a huge company, when it is in fact only a fraction of the population of Serpentin.

Next, I reverently pick the capsule up, cradling it in my arms as we make our way in procession to the capsule archives, where the capsule of every Serpentin who ever died rests. It is underneath the city, catacomb-like, with rows and rows of honeycomb holes in the walls for capsules. There is a separate section for Hydras and *Tradition Keepers*, the two highest ranks in the Serpentin hierarchy. I slot the hexagonal cylinder into a free spot, and I nod in respect. The congregation of mourners follows suit, despite some coveting Nada's now vacant position. I only said what they wanted to hear. I hardly knew her aside from her insatiable hunger and vindictive manner. I estimated that she must be around 60 in Serpentin years, which is correct, judging from her years of service. Only 30 in Earth years.

Now to business. We regroup in the atrium on the ground floor, gaining a number of lower-ranking soldiers, lending an ear to my appointment. Each secretly hoping that they are the chosen one. A podium is set up opposite the door, at the furthest wall, to provide room for the throng that is milling around, awaiting a revelation.

"Now, we must continue with the business of a new *Tradition Keeper*. I believe that I have elected the perfect person for the job…"
A couple of the officials are visibly salivating at the thought of all that power, disgusting creatures.
"They are not the archetypal candidate, nor the automatic choice. Their uniqueness will stand them in good stead."

Nervous shuffling and suspicious glances. I scan the room, squinting to see through the blizzard of Serpentins. Ah ha! There they are…

"Would Eimear please step up to the podium?"
A solidly built Serpentin woman pushes and shoves to get in front, smugly surveying her colleagues.
"Not you, Emer. My servant, Eimear."
An admiral grabs her behind the neck and drags her to me.
"Here you go. I caught her tiptoeing out of the room."

"Yes Hydra?" she cowers.
"Eimear, I have selected you to become the *Tradition Keeper*. You have proven that you are in fact the most knowledgeable in matters of law and order in the Serpentin Empire."
Her pupils dilate into saucer eyes, and she gazes at me, transfixed. Maybe even afraid.

"I call for an urgent reconsideration!" Someone bellows, rupturing the silence. "This decision must not stand! We will not have a non-Serpentin directing our affairs, we already have a half-breed leading the Empire. This is an outrage!"

"Excuse me, you will defer to the Hydra, sir."

"She is not fit to make this choice; she is not pure like us. The one she has chosen was her servant! A servant cannot become the *Tradition Keeper*!"

"Objection! I meet all qualifications for the role. The law does not mention the requirement of the *Tradition Keeper* to be Serpentin. I am well versed in the law and regulation, and I will not hesitate to enforce the law. That law includes the illegal nature of resisting the judgements of the Hydra and the *Tradition Keeper.* That entails the death penalty!" She springs into her part, as if she were in a play, pretending to be someone she isn't.

"Absurd! How would you, without the capabilities of a Serpentin, mete out such a punishment? You couldn't eat one of us."

"Why don't you just come up here then?"

I can see Eimear shaking with the exertion of projecting such confidence. Months of conditioning and training to be a servant has taken its toll on her self-esteem and self-perception. I smirk gleefully at who is being summoned. It is the Admiral from earlier, who gave me such attitude.

"What could you do to me? I am not afraid of a skinny little lunch like you!" he growls, the words seeming to seep from the back of his throat. Eimear's eyes falter, and her right-hand quavers like it does when she is scared.

"What could she do to you? She wouldn't have to eat you to inflict a mortal injury. She has the power to let you die slowly while you cadge and bargain."

My cheeks colour as I bluff, locking eyes with Eimear pleadingly. Please think of something, please...

"Hand me a knife," she states bluntly.

I ceremoniously present her with the dagger customarily given to the *Tradition Keeper*, often used to mark the servant set aside for the Hydra. Eimear has a long scar down her right forearm from Nada's blade.

"Now, where is the best place to cut for tenderness?"

"On a male, I would say, the back or the abdomen. You pick."

"Hmm…"

"Or the soles of the feet, or…"

"Please stop," he whimpers softly.

"Oh, it speaks! Wonders never cease," I quip sarcastically.

"I apologise for my insults and lack of respect. Truly, Hydra. Have mercy!" His voice alters to a nasal, higher register.

"The back. Turn around," Eimear ignores him.

He refuses, so I grip his shoulder and spin him around to face me, and away from Eimear. I stare him dead in the eye as Eimear pulls his uniform up to expose his back. Not the most attractive back, I'd imagine. He carries a bit too much weight around his middle. He winces as she runs the knife down his back, like you would when about to fillet a fish.

"I think, here?"

"Yes, that will do nicely," I peer around to examine the area.

"For what?" he panics.

Eimear commences slowly digging the blade in, making a very small incision. He grits his teeth and bites his tongue, blood crawling down his chin. As soon as I see blood, I know she will stop. Although excellent with all other aspects of medicine, Eimear is unable to cope with the sight of blood. The knife quivers in her hand as the tip reddens. She frowns, trying ever so hard to finish what she started. I stroll over to inspect her progress. I lean to whisper discreetly in her ear.

"You can stop if you want. Think of something else, think humiliating rather than gory."

"Thanks Jade… Umm… Hydra, Sorry."

"You know, I don't really feel like it anymore, the moment has passed. Stand to attention Admiral!" She withdraws, pulling his shirt down quickly so she doesn't have to see the little trickle of blood creeping down his back.

Her sudden change of volume makes him flinch. He salutes, eyes wary of Eimear. He is wise to exercise caution, for an angered *Tradition Keeper* is the most unpredictable kind. Even a Xenonian one. Eimear walks right up to him, facing him head on, staring him down. I find the spectacle hilarious, but I must remain composed and stone-faced. She is wracking her brains for options. I have seen her accidentally stare at me while she is thinking, and trust me, it is formidable. I forgive her though, mainly because I also have a furious "thinking face."

Abruptly, efficiently, she slaps him across the face, leaving an angry red mark on his milky skin. Lacking any outward display of frustration, she turns and stands beside me. We watch him like seabirds scan the water, poised to dive at any hint of fish below. He does not look back, he knows better. He clutches at what dignity he still possesses, and fades into the masses, no doubt to sulk somewhere. I signal to the servants on either side of the room to disperse the crowds, and the ceremony is complete.

"I applaud your icy composure. You were superb."

"I hated it. Although, admittedly, I did rather enjoy slapping that Admiral in the face."

"Haha, that was solid entertainment. You will grow into the role. I eventually might settle in mine."

"Don't get too comfortable Jade, lest you forget your Illumaen side."

"You will remind me Eimear. You went from a servant with an appalling stutter and various nervous ticks, to the *Tradition Keeper*. You are eloquent, learned, and gentle. You will go far as my advisor."

"I hope further than Nada..."

"Well, the key to not ending up like Nada is not going behind my back and planning invasions on planets we have peace treaties with," I grin.

"I will keep that in mind," she giggles sweetly.

"Where are we going?" she queries, as if she had only just realised that we are walking.

"To your new quarters."

"Wait, what?"

"Here we are."

"Nada's quarters? I am going to live here??"

Nada's quarters are plush, elegant and kept scrupulously clean by her servant, who we find asleep on the floor. I bet nobody told her that Nada was dead, so she just continued with her work.

"I am going to live here... Really? What about you??" she gasps, astounded.

"You are free, Eimear. You now have your own servant, and your own quarters for the duration of your life."

"How? What did I do to deserve this great privilege?"

"You are the most intelligent woman I have ever had the honour of knowing. You are the most suitable to advise me. It was only logical."

I resist saying "the most intelligent non-Illumaen," due to the arrogant ring of the phrase. I hand her a small document legally declaring that I have granted her freedom. Her face lights up, and she beams excitedly.

"So, what will you do first with your newfound power Eimear?"

"Oh, I am not really sure. What can I do?"

"You can advise me to capture or free any planet or people, within reason. Make sure it is a sensible action, one which fortifies the Empire."

"Xenon?"

"Oh, Xenon. What about it?" I question playfully.

"Can you free my people?"

"That would take at least a week's coordination. The population likely does not have much of a chance if someone gets wind of the operation. What do we need to do first?"

I draw her out skilfully. It is imperative for her to master this line of reasoning.

"A moratorium on taking slaves from there until we can organise terms with the planet."

"Exactly. Go, declare the moratorium on taking slaves from Xenon. As soon as you have settled of course…"

"Oh, I will! Let me leave my bag inside; I will be with you momentarily."

"I will allow you to do this on your own."

"Oh…" Now she doesn't sound so sure.

In spite of this, she needs the training if she is to be the second highest in the Empire. My subjects require considerable bossing around to get used to changes.

Just then, Nada's servant leaps up, her skin turning grey in fear. Upon seeing that it is not Nada, it returns to its natural green colour. She is covered in scales like a Chameleon, able to blend in with the background. I almost tripped over her when I walked into the living room, although thankfully I spotted her in time. Her hands and feet have sticky pads like a Gecko, but she stands on two legs, coming to Eimear's waist level. Nada had her for a whole week and a half, so either she is the best servant who ever lived, or Nada didn't want to eat a Gecko-Chameleon half-sized Humanoid.

"Meet your new mistress, 64582."

"The Hydra? It shall be an honour to serve you."

"No, the *Tradition Keeper* Her name is Eimear."

"I greet you humbly, my mistress."

"Call me Eimear."

"I will leave you two to become acquainted, while I search for a new servant. I hope you succeed in your assignment."

"Yes Hydra. Thank you, Hydra."

She is practically the perfect *Tradition Keeper*. Polite, submissive, but with excellent suggestions and ideas.

With that, I make my way to the slave market, to find somebody else to keep my quarters.

The Old Fades, the New Rises

Two Serpentin weeks (twelve days) later, at nearly midday, I emerge from my quarters, bedecked in the outfit I donned for my *Installation*. The poor seamstress really tried to make it fit, but eventually she had to capitulate. All she had to do was release the ribbon by two or three inches at the top. It is only when I step onto the silver carpet and glance down, that I observe a difference. The bodice is acting as a push-up bra, uncomfortably so. How did I miss that? In the textbooks I had read of this phenomenon. Serpentins start to mature between the ages of 20 and 28 (10 and 14 on Earth), but they have a second maturation when they reach 36 to 40. I guess that happened rather quickly. My usual style is more relaxed in fit, so I never fully appreciated the change in my shape. Only now do I recognise the wisdom of such a flattering neckline. So distracted am I by my own chest that I almost walk straight past the Illumaens lurking on the side lines.

"*Polypterus Senegalis* Jade, most exalted Hydra."

"Greetings. Have you come to belittle me for being too Serpentin? This is neither the time nor the place."

"No, we have not daughter." My Father gently moves a couple of people aside to clear himself a space in front of the throng. "I wished to personally praise the changes you are to enact today."

"Many thanks, however only time will heal the wound the Society inflicted on me. The humiliation alone is enough to put one off."

"We have been considering that a hiatus in your ambassadorial work may be mutually beneficial."

"But I am amply qualified, I can handle potentially explosive situations..."

"We know Jade," another in the delegation chips in.

"May our philosophies keep pace with our power," Lawrence muses ponderously.

"Sorry? I do not understand your meaning."

"It means, that we cannot let our influence or power affect who we really are. Once you learn to handle the sway you have on Serpentin, you may return to your Illumaen role. Given your behaviour in the last meeting of the Council, the authority is beginning to go to your head. On Illuma, your opinion is not the highest in the Union. You must respect the system before you can become a part of it. When I first met you, you were humble, gentle, accommodating. These qualities are valued in the Society. Outspokenness, and interrupting others, are not."

"Hmm... That is reasonable. I do have difficulty balancing my Serpentin and Illumaen sides. When I can discover a stable compromise between the two, I will return to prove myself a worthy Ambassador once more."

"So we are on the same plane of thought - excellent. I wish you good fortune in transforming both yourself and the Serpentin Empire."

"Thank you. Good day," I shake hands with him before continuing down the silver path.

As I elegantly float up the three steps to the platform, I turn my head to the right, recognising a flash of white iridescence out of the corner of my eye. Diamond is standing a little way back, and I can just about catch a glimpse of Electra's head bobbing beside her. I raise a hand, hold it motionless momentarily, and return it to my side. Waving is not very Serpentin, or Illumaen. Finally, I have uncovered a similarity concealed by their astounding disparity. Diamond reciprocates, and Electra flails both hands most inappropriately at me. A soft smile plays on my lips, before I turn away and continue to the podium. The platform is smack in the middle of the Platz, with a maelstrom of Serpentins surrounding it. Quite a different set up in comparison to my *Installation*. There is a stationary voice amplifier connected to the podium, but instead I fiddle with my earpiece until I activate a modification I have been working on for the past week. I like to walk the stage while speaking.

"Greetings citizens, servants, and guests of the Serpentin Empire!" The almost invisibly thin wire curved around my cheek, with a nano-microphone attached on the end, projects my voice with stunning clarity.

As I had hoped, the chaos subsides. All in the sea of people fall silent, standing stock-still. I exchange an impressed glance with Eimear, who is stationed beside me.

"I am well aware of the confusion, perhaps even the concern, experienced by all with regard to these legislative adjustments. I shall be discussing two changes to our laws. Firstly, the doubling of the price of a slave. And secondly, the introduction of different species to be bred for food, along with the protocols surrounding this. For each of these new directives, I will explain: 1. How this will affect the way we manage our resources, and 2. The ultimate benefit to the Empire resulting from these changes."

"The Hydra is wholly committed to maintaining the powerful reach and formidable dominance of our Empire. We shall remain the most feared species in the Galaxy!" Eimear shouts militaristically to back me up.

"To power!" I reinforce. The assembly erupts with the tremendous racket of concurrence.

I pace impatiently to hush the raucous of the crowd, before conveying my next thought.

"To begin, the price of a slave. The fact is, that we are fast running out of slaves. The turnover is unacceptable. It is unnatural to go through one or two slaves a week - after all, they do all the hard work around here. If we keep them for longer, they could be more efficient in their duties, and reduced fear would be a huge advantage. The price will double. Half of the price goes to the trader, as before, so your business will not be affected in terms of profit per slave. A quarter goes to the government, and the last quarter of the price is given to the slave, or their next of kin."

"But why? Our slaves have no need of money; we provide for their needs!" An annoyed man shouts.

"True, but this is for a different purpose. It means that if they wish, they can buy their freedom. However, they need to earn back their full value, and negotiate with you, the owner. You are still completely in control. If, for example, you had a servant who has been loyal for years. Always obedient, obliging, industrious. However, they have aged, and are growing less useful. You are entitled to ask for their quarter of the price you paid, in return for their freedom. You must write them a signed document stating that they are now free. Any flouting the law, or cheating their slaves, will personally be punished by me, with maximum severity."

"Now, on to the benefits gleaned by the Empire. More loyal slaves mean fewer rebellions within our dominion. Parents are given the opportunity to have more children, sell them to us, and use the portion they receive to buy their freedom. Four children are worth the freedom of one parent. A decreased mortality rate would further encourage this system, along with the hope of liberty. We have a consistent flow of slaves, and some slaves can eventually be freed, to serve as beacons of hope for the majority to aspire to. The slaves will work harder, as they have a positive incentive to please, rather than solely the threat of being consumed."

"The second matter to be addressed is the use of non-humanoid species as food. This practice is both common and reasonably satisfactory on Earth, and Electrolaia. I have already sourced quadrupeds from Titanium, a moon of Electrolaia. Over the past week I have stayed on the farm, accompanied by the *Tradition Keeper* and some soldiers, to learn the methods of breeding, raising and slaughtering the organisms."

Everybody pricks their ears up when they hear "slaughtering" enter the equation.

"The soldiers previously assigned to conquering new planets from the ground, will now farm these invaluable sources of food."
"What are they? They sound like servants, only we kill them differently," a crowd member pipes up.

"On Earth humans dub them "livestock." They are living things with a more primitive language than us. They act primarily on instinct rather than possessing complex reasoning. We would indeed kill them differently. It is more humane to kill the animal before eating it. Humans often cook the meat prior to consumption, with added flavourings to increase their enjoyment of the food."

"The entire objective of eating our prey alive is to strike terror into the hearts of our enemies. Can we not continue that with this "livestock," as you call it?"

"The animal would not understand the threat as you would like them to. It simply would not be the same. Therefore, it is better to kill the animal first, then apportion the meat between the members of your household. They are substantial beasts, capable of feeding four or five Serpentins. Their fodder is reasonably priced, and I now have an army of people trained to handle them. The price per animal will be half that of a slave. In fact, out of my generosity as Hydra, each household will receive an animal free of charge. A soldier will come to assist you in butchering and preparing it."

I am positive that the Illumaen delegation is grimacing right now. I am inwardly cringing. Of course, animals are different to humans, but that does not make it okay to eat them. I believe that, especially as I try to be vegetarian. Nevertheless, this is the lesser of the two evils. This is only the beginning of a long road to reform. I must bear that in mind, through all the setbacks and obstacles. I will leave this Empire in a much better state than when I found it. I will produce a more educated, open-minded Empire. It just requires a huge amount of leg work and effort. Not to mention, dodging assassins.

"So, how is this going to improve the Empire?" The irritating person in the audience butts in again.

"In order to pull this off, we must form alliances with neighbouring planets to source fodder and stock." I continue, unfazed. "I have re-deployed another section of our infantry to mine part of Palladium for valuable elements, to trade with. We can go about extending our influence at a more leisurely pace, not at the absurd breakneck speed of desperation we went at previously. We shall have a sustainable supply of slaves, as we will not be as reliant on them to feed us. The army can be reduced, so there is no longer the requirement of mandatory conscription. Instead, young Serpentins may choose to be educated in an area of interest. I plan to construct centres of learning for young children aged 6 and upwards."

"So you see, citizens of Serpentin, our most exalted Hydra has grand plans for the Empire. She plans to make your children more intelligent, more knowledgeable, making us not only a military force, but an intellectual one. Why, we may even be in a position to compete with the Illumaen Union!" Eimear shouts defiantly.

At this point I frown a warning at her, considering the delegation standing nearby.

"We will rise to fame and greatness we never even dreamed of!"

"Yes, to fame, greatness, and the formidable Empire!" I forge the motto by which I will reign henceforth.

"To fame, greatness, and the formidable Empire!" The ecstatic crowd cheers. Eimear looks at me, and I her.

"We've done it," I whisper proudly.

"We certainly have. No - you certainly have, Hydra."

The hushed reply floats across to me with an echo of Eimear's radiant, joyful smile. We have done it. Taken that first step; and succeeded.

Printed in Great Britain
by Amazon

54178670R00115